QUARANTINE DAYS

An anthology curated by

VAISHALI CHANDORKAR CHITALE

Inkfeathers Publishing
www.inkfeathers.com

Quarantine Days
Edited & compiled by
Vaishali Chandorkar Chitale
Print Edition

First Published in India in 2022
Inkfeathers Publishing
New Delhi 110095

Copyright © Inkfeathers Publishing, 2022

ISBN 9789390882052

www.inkfeathers.com

Disclaimer

The anthology 'Quarantine Days' is a collection of 28 stories and 10 poems written by 28 authors who belong to different parts of India.

Unless otherwise indicated, all the names, characters, objects, businesses, places, events, incidents—whether physical/non-physical, real/unreal, tangible/ intangible in whatsoever description used in this book are either the product of the author's imagination or used in a fictitious manner. Any resemblance to actual persons, objects, entities, living or dead, or actual events is purely coincidental.

The stories published in this book are solely owned by their respective authors and are in no way intended to hurt anyone's religious, political, spiritual, brand, personal or fanatic beliefs and/or faith, whatsoever. In case, any sort of plagiarism is detected in the stories within this anthology or in case of any complaints or grievances or objections, neither the anthology editor nor the publisher is to be held responsible.

Dedicated to

All of us

Who survived the pandemic

With fear in our hearts but a smile on our lips.

Contents

About the Editor

An optimist to the core, Vaishali Chandorkar Chitale always sees the glass half full. She firmly believes in the saying, 'Hope is the most exciting thing there is in life.' An alumna of the Indian Institute of Mass Communication (Journalism), New Delhi, she is a freelance journalist, a poet, and a writer. Her poems and stories have been published on various online platforms and she has won many certificates for the same.

She has regularly contributed to both the Inkfeathers Publishing and Impish Lass Publishing House and her stories have been published in fifteen of their anthologies. She is also a freelance editor and has successfully conceptualised and co-edited an anthology for ILPH, 'Women vs We Men' and 'Second Innings' and one for Inkfeathers Publishing, 'Marital Games'. She is presently conceptualising and editing two more anthologies for both the publishing houses.

Her story 'Bittersweet Chocolate' was ranked third in an exclusively for-women-writers contest, held by Writefluence in 2020, and was published in their book "Out of my BOX", available on Amazon, in paperback and eBook editions. Her winning story, 'All That Glitters…' has been published in Out of my BOX-II, in 2022.

She has also won in the contests "High Five" and "Sonnetto" held by Writefluence for poets. Her winning poems have been published in their books of poems, "Tickled Pink" and "Standstill". She has also won in story writing contests and has been featured in their books, "Mrs. Rosewood", "Rubble House" and "A Lie on Her Lips".

Her story, 'A Road Not Taken', came 6th amongst more than 500 entries on Story Mirror for which she won a certificate and a reward. Her stories, "Menage-A-Trois" and "Raison D' Etre" have won a medal and a certificate each in the third prize category in the Asian Literary Society's Annual Wordsmith Award, 2021, Short Story contest. Her winning poems and stories have been published in their Anthology of Stories, 2021.

She came first in a poetry contest held by Write fluence on World Poetry Day, 2022 and was awarded a trophy for the same. Her co-authored coffee table book on poems, "Poets and Poems-Echoes" has been published recently to rave reviews.

She is a member of Women's Indian Chamber of Commerce and Industry (WICCI) Maharashtra (Special Needs) for the year 2021-22.

She has taught English in many schools and retired from Delhi Public school, Pune in 2004 after a career of over 14 years to pursue her passion for writing. She lives in Mumbai with her family. You can follow her on her blog www.anenviablejourney.wordpress.com. She can be reached at vchandorkar@gmail.com.

Editor's Note

Quarantine, lockdown, pandemic... these words were unheard of till two years back. Happy in our pursuits, we were cruising along on our chosen paths, till our juggernaut was rudely stopped by a minuscule coronavirus in early 2020. Shaped like a crown, it was anything but; whoever came within its reach, had to be isolated and quarantined—at home or otherwise.

We were stopped in our tracks, literally. Overnight, the world came to a standstill. The busy roads, offices, marketplaces, shopping malls, theatres, et al., were as if covered by a shroud and the cities and mofussil areas, busy metropolises till a day back turned into ghostly towns.

Quarantine turned our lives upside down. Till now, used to a day or two off in a week, we suddenly found ourselves all days of the week home. Initial euphoria led to boredom and frustration when the actual 'work-from-home' took on a different meaning—we had to be available at any time of the day, as we were working from home!

Though we all were under one umbrella—Quarantine—but each one of us has had our individual journeys, each one of us dealt with the crisis in our own unique way and most of us emerged victorious, we all are the winners here, we have all gone through a harrowing time and emerged victors: some not entirely unscathed, but winners none the same.

This book is an attempt to encapsulate these very stories; stories of how everyone dealt with the lockdown—sometimes downbeat and pessimistic; sometimes upbeat and optimistic—but undoubtedly these past two years will go down in the history of mankind as the most unprecedented event of the century.

Stories of hope, valour, optimism, tongue-in-cheek humour—the book has them all. Some stories will break your heart while some will make you chuckle with nostalgia.

We hope that this anthology resonates with you and brings back forgotten memories—some happy, some-not-so-happy... but one thing is for sure, these stories will leave an imprint on your mind and stay with you for a long time.

So, dear readers, without further ado, let me leave you to read this anthology in peace and enjoy the collection of heart-warming stories and sweet lyrical poems that we present before you.

Happy Reading!
Vaishali Chandorkar Chitale

Deleted

@Anjali Dalal

'Sorry, Mummy!' 'Sorry, Mummy!' 'Sorry, Mummy!' 'Sorry...' Shrill crying. Shrieking. Persistent crying. More crying. Sobbing. Now silence. A very long one. Couple of hours long.

Trring! Trring! Trring! She goes cycling. Tricycling to be precise. Her grandfather in toe. To the park.

Radha. The child lives two houses away, and yet I hear her. Clearly. Most mornings. She hates bathing. Or so they keep saying. Her mother drags her to it. I think. She resists. Boom! The slap. I think that's how it goes. I don't like to hear her cry. Apologising. Sobbing. Repeat.

She is all of four earth years old. She is apologising. I'm sure she doesn't know why. Maybe, she wants to see her Mummy smile again. Like the times when she was a suckling baby. The times when her entire world rested on her Mummy. Her smile. Her cooing. Her gaze. Her smell. Her touch. She may have stared at her mother for hours. That's the comfort she craves. Wait. I need to think deeper. This is important to me. I too belong to the category of human children. Her Mummy slaps her. She cries. I don't like that.

What wrong has she done? Why does her Mummy force her to have a bath? Or have a bath at all? Why can't she play longer?

Other children are still playing in the park. Can she not play on the see-saw? And the slide, too? Why does her resistance meet the unmistakable slap? What about her individuality? Is it not numbed into silence? By the very person who should nurture it the most? Why do grown-ups hurt children? Is it because children can't hit back? Why do grown-ups make children if they don't like them? Why do grown-ups keep saying they don't have time? Hurry up! Hurry up! Hurry up! Don't they know children are all about time? Can children be pushed around like furniture? Is it because grown-ups don't understand how to raise children? Don't they know children come without a how-to-raise-me manual?

My head hurts. Dizzy. Dizzy. Dizzy. Too many questions. Enough to put me over the edge. I need sleep.

Whirr! Whirr! Whirr! For heaven's sake! That's too loud. Such a racquet. The noisy juicer! Gulp. Gulp. Gulp. But it makes tasty juice. My Ma specially makes it for me. How does she know I like it? I haven't told her that. But the green juice in the mornings is yucky! This one is sweet. I love it. And I know I am loved. Loved. And deeply so. Ever since I was a zygote.

Vroom! Vroom! Vroom! Car ride. Yippee! Tumbling up and down. Up and down. The car is filled with music. Ma sings, 'La Lala la Lala la Lala.' The music system blares:

Wheels on the bus go round and round

round and round

round and round

The wheels on the bus go round and round

All through the town

Honk! Honk! Brake. Our first halt. The boutique for Ma's clothes. Ma is in double good mood. Ma asks after her new dress.

The boutique lady doesn't answer right away. Swirls in talks. Lot of talks. Fabric. Colour. Texture. Embroidery. Buttons. Matching *"potli"* (purse). Contrasting *"nakki"* (embellishments). Length of *"kurta"* (upper women's garment). Silhouette of *"shalwar"* (lower women's garment). Trending fashion. Traffic problems. Terrific weather. *'Yeh burfi khaaiye. Bhaiyyoo ke chachaa ki shaadi ki hain.* (Do eat these sweets. They are from my brother-in-law's marriage celebrations.)' Ma refuses politely.

She begins her verbal diarrhoea. Again. Excuses tumble out. For not stitching Ma's clothes. Been quite unwell. Boutique shut. For more than two weeks. She can hardly pull herself out of bed. Still can't eat enough food. Too weak to work. Too much pending work. Her two teenage sons manage household chores. She nearly died. Not because of the C Virus. *'Maine toh DNC karwa li thi. Bus lahparwaahi ho gayi. Chaar mahine upar ho gaye. Woh bhi ladki.* (I underwent an abortion. I was negligent and didn't use protection. The foetus was four months old. A female foetus.)'

Silence. Eerie. Thunderbolt-infused. Voices in the background. Ma finally mumbles something. I can't hear her. I hear Lub-dub, lub-dub, lub-dub. Ma's heart. Beating fast. No. Frantic. We walk back to the car. Hurriedly. Fast. Very fast. Now we run. The lub-dub lub-dub getting louder. Finally in the car. No music this time. Just the lub-dub lub-dub. We zip away. We reach home. Maid runs to open the door. Ma drinks water. Too much water. She should rest. Ma needs to listen to her doctor. Less work. No worry.

121.7475 days is equal to four months. Womb age. The boutique lady deleted her child. Deleted! Ball and chain release.

What wrong did Deleted Child do? Big mischief? Did she not obey her mother like Radha did? Was the mother punishing her? Could she not just slap the child but let her live? Like Radha's mother? Can mothers delete? Children. So why create us? If they want to delete. Children. Did Deleted Child feel the pain? How did they do it? Knife? Poison? Did the child cringe with fear? Did she curl her fingers? Or her toes? Did she cry for help? Did the mother hear the child cry? But then who would help if the mother wanted to delete? Why did the mother not hear? The cries. The helpless squiggling. The terrified heartbeats. Thud. Thud. Thud. Thudthudthud… Thuthuthu… Ththth… Hhhhhh…

Tears mixed in blood. Red. Vermilion. Scarlet.

17.381 weeks. Deleted baby's age. Two-week-old womb baby's heart begins to beat. The doctor said. The one Ma visits. Deleted baby's heart must be strong at 17.381 weeks. But not strong enough. Not strong enough for the knife. Not strong enough for the poison.

Where did her soul go? Did it go back to God? What about the body? Deleted Child's? Where is it? Where did the tears mixed in blood go? Will God love her? Did anyone ever love her? Oh, the poor dear!

Boutique lady didn't talk about Deleted Child. No kind words. No fond memory. Only gossip. Trivial. Meaningless. Unhappy for not feeling well. Unhappy for not eating well. Unhappy for business not doing well. No. Not a word. Nothing in the name of an obituary.

Oh, you nameless poor dear! Unloved. Unwanted. Oh, how I wish you had chosen another womb! Of the lady who visits Ma's doctor. The one who is desperately waiting. For a child. For a miracle.

Deleted Child found a home in an unwelcome womb. Even so. Mother-child bond was forged. Mother did have a duty towards the child. But. But no. Mother chose to be evil. Chose to be selfish. Chose to not choose the child. Chose to forget 'Karma.'

Ma reads to me every night. From the Bhagavad Gita. Ma talks of the principle of Karma. The eternal science of right action. Every thought and action have corresponding reactions. The universe responds to you sooner or later. According to the quality of your actions. Karma is a store of good and bad actions, accumulated over many lives. Selfless actions uplift a human. Selfish actions degrade a human. The results of both actions are experienced over a series of lifetimes.

Ma reads about three kinds of Karmas. Sanchita (latent Karma), Prarabdha (ripened Karma), and Agami (future Karma). Sanchita is accumulated Karma from past thoughts and actions, the result of which will be experienced in the future. Sanchita is like the seed of a tree you planted in the past. The tree will grow and produce a particular fruit you're destined to eat.

Prarabhdha is what you're experiencing now. It is the seed of the past action that has grown into a tree, producing the fully ripened fruit you are eating in the present.

Agami is the seed of action you're planning in the present that will produce the fruit in future.

I recall Ma singing one verse in particular:

shri bhagavan uvacha

partha naiveha namutra vinashas tasya vidyate

na hi kalyana-krit kashchid durgatim tata

gachchhati

The Bhagavad Gita: Chapter 6, Verse 40:

Ma translates it thus: The Supreme Lord said, 'O Parth! One who engages on the spiritual path does not meet with destruction either in this world or in the world to come. My dear friend, one who strives for God, realisation is never overcome by evil.' So, if one takes karmic lessons seriously, and strives to act selflessly, one can continuously elevate one's status of existence. One cannot be vanquished by evil. If, however, a human chooses to commit one selfish act after another, spiritual progress is not made. In extreme cases, what progress has already been made can be squandered.

Ma says God is watching us from his home in Heaven. Did He see the bad Karma? Will He punish Deleted Child's mother?

I'm now sure of one thing. Better be deleted than be unloved. No one to love hurts. Harder. That's why Radha cries. I think. Loud. Heartfelt. Gut wrenching cries. Her mother's slap stings her. The pain rendered is less by the slap. More by the sight of her mother. Angry. Unforgiving. Unloving.

Whoosh! Whoosh! Whoosh! Motherly fluid. Synonym for Ma's love. Informs me that I'm surrounded with love. They call me Bubbles. Yes. I know. It's a plural name. I don't even have a twin. Ma and Baba say I bring them bubbles of happiness. That's why I'm Bubbles. Unisex name. They are busy these days. Redecorating the nursery. New theme. New colour. It was pink and blue for my sister. In case baby turned out to be a boy. Now its pink and myriad shades of green.

Trips to market. Window shopping. Choosing. Buying. New clothes. New toys. New books.

Ma and Baba whisper sometimes about hard times. Quarantine. The lockdown. Things getting expensive. So, will they? No. They won't. Or will they? Delete me too?

No. No. Not at all. I am way too loved. I'm swaddled in warm fluid-filled membranes. Still attached to my Ma's umbilical cord. Literally. Ma sits on the garden swing, soaking in the early morning sun. Meditation and yoga make her happy. She sips a tasty juice and strokes me lovingly. A few more days. Then I will see her and the world with my very own eyes. I'm all of eight and-a-half womb months old.

Inflammable

@Rudra Narayan Dash

This story has been inspired by true events.

'*Are we going to the amusement park tomorrow?*'

The distant words echoed in Rajpal's mind. His only family—his son, had made a request. And yet again, he could not fulfil it. He cursed himself as he walked through the narrow streets of his town, flooded by the drains. The marshy water covered the roads everywhere. Walking without slipping was almost impossible. His house, a dilapidated shelter, was the only roof he could put together for himself and his son.

I must get the money for Ashok, he thought as he jumped over a puddle of dirty water. Dressed in his regular old shirt and pants, he unconsciously checked his pockets to come up with at least some money. After getting fired from the firecracker merchant's factory, he wondered if he even had enough to arrange a meal for tonight.

Keeping the pandemic in mind, the government recently banned the sales of firecrackers. The burning vapours of sulphur and nitrogen were harmful to the already weak lungs, they said. By the time the news reached the factories, it was too late. The firecrackers were reduced to nothing. Seeing this, the merchant in a paranoid frenzy, fired all of his workers, suppliers, and manufacturers without paying them a single dime—all in one night.

How could he? The feeling of dread still lingered in Rajpal. But as cruel as the situation was, he could not blame his boss for this sudden onset of misfortune upon him.

'Morality seldom wins in a fight against desperation.'

He didn't have any money to provide the salaries to the scores of people working in his factory. Rajpal wondered if his boss had enough to even feed himself. But he shook the thoughts away as he became more and more aware of the uncertainty of his future. This was not the time to worry about others.

He stood in front of the door to his house, a flap that he had fished out from the garbage dump. He had washed it with some water and sewn it using his neighbour's sewing machine. He took a deep breath and entered the house, ready to face his son.

As he entered, he found his son on the floor, doodling on a piece of paper. It was cold. The boy was wearing a full-sleeved shirt, riddled with holes and tattered cargo pants. With him was the small, framed picture of his mother, smiling.

Once again, I come home empty-handed, Yimmi.

'Shomu,' he called. The little boy turned his head at him and immediately rushed to him. 'Papa! Papa!' he said as he hugged his father. Rajpal hugged his son as tightly as he could. It felt heavenly to be embraced by such an innocent and pure soul. All the weariness, dejection, and the loss he felt during the entirety of the day, washed away like sand on a beach.

'Papa! Papa!' Shomu squealed as his father put him down and headed over to the sink.

'Hmm?'

'Are we going to the amusement park tomorrow?'

Rajpal froze as he heard the words. He phased out for a moment before snapping back to the present, seeing the boy looking at him.

'It's a surprise,' he said with a half-smile.

'Surprise!? Yay! Yay! We are going to the amusement park!' said Ashok as he started jumping.

'We… We are not going to the amusement park.'

Ashok stopped jumping, and his smile dropped. He sat down, looking at his father after hearing the same line again.

Rajpal, noticing the sudden change in his boy, wiped his hands on a cloth and sat down near him. As he reached out for the boy's arm, he slapped it back angrily. Rajpal exhaled slowly, bracing himself for what was going to happen.

'Shomu, you are a big boy now. And big boys don't act so stubborn!' he said, trying to calm his son down.

'But Chintu is going! His dad is going to take him tomorrow. It would be amazing if I could go with him. We will visit the same rides; eat the same food; buy the same toys.'

'Don't you know what's happening? There is a monster outside! If he sees more than three people at one place, something bad will happen!' Rajpal tried to scare his boy.

At first, Ashok didn't appear convinced. But when his father showed him how the demon roamed outside, looking for prey, fear slowly crept into his innocent little heart.

'What will happen if he sees more than three people?' he asked, curious and afraid at the same time.

Rajpal got silent for a moment, grabbed his son's shoulders, and shook them. 'You will get sick! You will cough, sneeze uncontrollably. You won't be able to breathe. You won't be able to sleep! Do you still want to go outside?'

'No… But…'

Rajpal let go of his son. He walked to the cupboard and took out his only tattered bag. He set it down and started putting their meagre amount of clothes in it.

The boy got up and ran to his father. 'Papa! Papa! What are you doing?'

'I am packing. We need to be prepared.'

'For what? Are we going somewhere?'

'Yes. We are going to the amusement park.'

'But you said there is a monster outside! We can't go!'

Rajesh stopped packing and looked at his son. 'I thought you wanted to go because Chintu was going.'

The little boy looked down at his feet and nervously replied, 'I… we will go some other time,' and walked away.

The only monster here is me, not the disease outside, Rajpal cursed at himself. Being unable to provide the happiness his son deserved was a nightmare on its own, let alone lying to him, again.

As he put the clothes back where they belonged, a small pouch fell out of the corner of the cupboard, making a jingling sound as it fell. The rustling must have shaken it up a bit. Rajpal picked up the pouch and opened it. Numerous coins with a few notes of money, lockets, bottle caps, and other trash. This wasn't his pouch; the texture was soft. He didn't know if it was velvet or leather, but he knew a poor man like him won't be able to afford something like this.

'Shomu.'

The boy turned to him and upon seeing the pouch in his father's hand, he turned his head back, trying to avoid father's soul-piercing gaze.

'Shomu, look at me. This isn't mine. The pouch and the money—how did it get here?' Rajpal slowly walked towards his son.

The boy remained silent as if someone had held him by his throat.

'I asked you something, Shomu. How did this get here?'

The boy didn't say a thing. Rajpal, fearing the worst, grabbed the boy by his arms and shook him hard.

'Shomu, did you steal this?' Rajpal asked his son, waiting for the bitter revelation.

The little boy put his head down, hesitating to answer his father.

'No,' he replied a few moments later.

'Then how did you get this?' The father snapped, angry at his son's denial. 'Have you started lying to me now!?'

'No! Papa! I am not lying!'

'THEN HOW IS THIS HERE!?' said Rajpal angrily.

Tears slowly rolled down the boy's cheeks. Everything fell silent. No cars whizzed past outside. No bottles were smashed in the neighbour's house. It was as if time almost stood still.

'I…' the boy started, 'I picked it up.'

'Picked? From where?' said the father surprised. This was unexpected.

'Yes, Papa. One day, when I came back home, I saw you crying while hugging Mama's picture and saying, 'I am sorry,' over and over again. That day I decided instead of staying at home, I would go out to the footpath and collect anything that is lying on the floor. That way I could help you, since you said nothing is useless in this world. But I didn't steal anything, I swear!'

The pouch fell from Rajpal's hand. Shomu flinched momentarily, but a few seconds later, gently embraced his father. Rajpal looked up as if trying to reach out to the heavens.

God, if you are there, I just want you to know. I don't want anything from you. But please do not let my boy worry about money. His little shoulders are too weak to handle it, he thought, unable to hold back his tears.

The Next Morning

'Rajpal! Rajpal!' A man called, outside Rajpal's house.

Rajpal opened his flap to see his fellow workmate, Nilesh.

'What's the matter? Did something happen?' he asked Nilesh, who was gasping for air, his mask dangling by his ear.

'The owner!' he said as he took deep breaths. 'He has called us back!'

'What?' remarked Rajpal surprised, 'I thought we were fired.'

'No, no!' said Nilesh hurriedly, 'After the government's verdict, huge orders have come in! Apparently, there are people who are still trying to buy firecrackers! They said something about a protest but who cares? We will have jobs!' Nilesh said, smiling widely.

Rajpal couldn't believe what he had just heard. He sat down from the weight of the sudden revelation, but his friend didn't give him time to think.

'Hey! Hey! Don't sit! Come quick! We need to go, right now! If we reach before the assembly starts, we will get 5 rupees extra per hour! Now, I am going ahead. Don't be late,' Nilesh screamed happily as he ran off.

The neighbour's doors opened, and a father-and-son duo stepped out in clean, crisp clothes.

'To the amusement park! Yay!' Chintu jumped up and down while holding his father's hand. The man, although struggling to lock the door, couldn't help but share his son's excitement. Suddenly, the boy turned around and noticed Rajpal looking at them. He rushed towards him, arms flailing.

'Rajpal Uncle! We are going to the park today!' the boy jumped up and down.

'Oh?' Rajpal laughed as he tried to hold the boy. 'And what are you going to buy?'

'Rides! Toys! I will buy everything!'

Rajpal watched as the duo disappeared at the corner of the street. He could still hear the little boy's happy squeals echo down the empty street.

He shot up from his chair with new determination. As he stood there under the morning sun, he found his son sleeping peacefully, and right beside his head was his mother's picture, ever smiling and beautiful.

I am sorry, Yimmi. I won't cry again. Not until I get out of this, he thought as he ran off to the owner's house.

'Do not be afraid of the seas, o' brave sailor.
Do not be afraid of the battlefield, o' brave soldier.
For the seas may rage, and the battlefield may quake.
But never be afraid, because the warrior inside lies,
desperate to awake.'

—Anonymous

Quarantine Learnings

@Kirti V

Questioning our mental stability,
Urging us to stay calm.
Appealing for the world to not to be negative,
Reassuring that it is doable.
Appreciating our concern for the universe,
Navigating through the
Testing times of life and
Inflicting a sense of fear,
Nursing everyone at home and
Emerging victorious against the virus.

Quarantine taught us to be strong by,
Ushering positive thoughts and deeds,
Applying the balm of love and care
Resting in the prayers of the world.
Acknowledging the service of others and
Nurturing hidden talents,
Teaching us to be united and strong.
Inducing the sense of brotherhood amongst
Near and far and the unseen too,
Enduring it was! But fruitful though.

For A Breath of Fresh Air

@Arun Hariharan

*For the fate of the sons of men and the fate of beasts is the same.
As one dies so dies the other; indeed, they all have the same breath
and there is no advantage for man over beast, for all is vanity.*

—*Ecclesiastes 3:19*

Amenla spooned up the oily chowmein and washed it down with sweet tea at the grubby food trolley below her lodging in the crowded urban village of Chakkarpur. With its crowded lanes, overflowing drains, squalid eating joints and matchbox like dwellings, Chakkarpur was a total antithesis of its rich cousin—Gurgaon's famous MG Road a.k.a. the mall-mile which was less than a kilometre away. Well, that's what the paradox of India's Cyber City was!

Amenla herself was a paradox in many ways. From far away Nagaland, a wannabe nurse at one point of time, leading a simple and happy life in the picturesque little town of Mokokchung, now less than two years hence, here she was, working fourteen hours a day in a beauty parlour in Sahara Mall and living in a damp and cramped room, which she shared with three other girls. From the time her father Jezebel, a schoolteacher, had suddenly died in a road accident a couple of years ago, life had not given her many choices. First, it was her dropping out of Nursing School, then doing a short beautician course and finally setting course for Delhi and picking up a beauty therapist's job in Gurgaon to support her mother and only sibling Joseph, who was spastic.

It had not been easy at all; in the beginning, the racial slurs, lewd comments, lecherous looks and groping by disgusting men got on to her and she used to cry herself to sleep each night; but over a period of time, she had got used to it. The only saving grace for all her hardship was that the money was reasonably good. She was able to earn upwards of twenty-five thousand rupees a month with her salary at the parlour and the occasional freelancing home visits she did for a few warmly acquainted women customers.

She entered her room and waved to Kanta, the Nepalese girl with whom she shared the room along with two others. The others were busy, glued to their mobiles with earphones plugged in. I don't know how these girls find the time and the energy, she wondered tiredly, and after changing to a comfortable tee and shorts, made a short call to her mother, Anung. As usual her mother was as cheerful as ever. Some woman she was—losing her husband suddenly, a spastic child in tow, and yet, she managed to stay cheerful, almost like a ray of sunlight seeping through dark clouds. Her mother was Amenla's strength and just talking to her made her forget all her worries and insecurities and made her work seem meaningful to her, in spite of all the hardship, extended working hours and occasional indignity she had to endure. The significant part of today's conversation was that she urgently had to send back home at least Rs 5,000 since her brother Joseph's therapy sessions were due at the hospital in Kohima in a few days.

Shabnam, the owner of the parlour and her employer, was not a great person, but she paid somewhat better than the others around (though she was invariably late in paying wages. The last month, that is, February's salary was yet to come in, even though it was almost end of March).

She suddenly heard yelling in the street below and could sense commotion. Kanta went down to check and came back with a look of shock on her face. 'Girls! Quick, let's stock something to eat… *Kal se kuch nahin milega* (you won't get anything from tomorrow),' she said. Amenla and the other two girls sat up, not able to comprehend what Kanta was saying. 'What happened? Will you tell us, or will you continue to blabber like a mad woman?' asked Ritu irritably, the Bihari girl.

'Modiji was on TV just now. There will be a complete lockdown across the city and the country for the next three weeks starting tomorrow morning. Can you believe it? Everything will be closed. No shops, no offices, no commotion on the road,' Kanta said, almost hysterically.

'You must be nuts. I'm sure you didn't hear it properly. Why would anyone do that?' Ritu retorted, perturbed.

Pushpa, the second Bihari girl, was now on an animated call with Arif, her boyfriend. She disconnected the call and turned to the others with an enlightened look on her face. 'The lockdown announcement by the PM is true. Haven't you guys heard about a new disease called Corona or something like that, which is spreading across the world like wild-fire and has no cure? It has started spreading in India, too; hence, the government has announced the closure of the whole country for some days.' The girls looked at each other in grave horror and trooped downstairs to the market to pick up a few meagre rations to stock up for a few days. They pooled in whatever little money they had and picked some rice, potatoes, and lentils. The shops were already swamped by anxious residents' overwhelming panic imbibed by frantic shopping for groceries and veggies.

A week and half went by, and it was well into April. Amenla was all alone in her dwelling now. The rest of the girls had scooted back to their villages by whatever means possible—buses and the handful of trains that were still running. But Amenla had very little choice. Shabnam had not paid her last month's salary and she still did not know what she would do back in Nagaland with no employment. Hence, she had decided to wait it out in Gurgaon. Of course, she was out of work now as the salon was closed and Shabnam had stopped taking her frantic calls asking for money. She had transferred her Rs 2,000 five days back but that was it. It was of course nice of her landlady, an old Bengali widow, who was okay with her paying delayed rent this month.

COVID had started spreading fast as was people's desperation. In the various news channels streaming into her mobile She could see graphic visuals of migrant workers literally walk it down to their villages in UP and Bihar, people from the North-East crowding into trains in Bangalore—in brief it seemed a hopeless situation. But it strengthened her resolve to stay on and wait out the storm, though she really longed to get back home in Mokokchung. Her mom and Joseph were fine so far— but they too needed money urgently.

It was 21st of April, and things began to get despairing for Amenla. The real bad news was that Shabnam had died of COVID a couple of days ago. She came to know when her daughter picked up the phone when Amenla called her for the nth time to enquire about her unpaid wages and also when they would be opening the salon. Her wages were definitely in the limbo now as the girl snapped back saying that she did not know anything about the accounts and how Amenla could even ask her all this when her mother had passed just two days ago.

April too went by. Her mother Anung had started sounding a little anxious now, the landlady, too, was a little less polite while reminding her for her overdue rent, her rations had practically run out and Shabnam's daughter had blocked Amenla's number. She felt like running away somewhere, but even that didn't seem feasible as the lockdown had been extended for two weeks more, and it was a fact that Nagaland was really far away.

Two mornings later, while she was staring into emptiness and contemplating what to do next, her phone suddenly rang and broke up her stupor. 'Why is Mrs Sethi calling me?' she wondered. Mrs Sethi was a middle-aged lady who stayed alone in a big house, Sushant Lok, and had been one of her regular home service customers.

'Hello! Yes, madam.' Amenla gingerly picked up the phone.

Mrs Sethi's voice at the other end sounded a little hoarse. '*Beta* (child), are you free?'

'Yes, of course. Thanks to the lockdown, I'm at my room only for the last many days,' said Amenla.

'Can you come over? I have some work for you,' said the voice at the other end.

'Sure, ma'am. When should I come, and would it be the usual?' she inquired.

'You can come at noon today and you may get your entire kit,' said Mrs Sethi.

Mrs Sethi was quite lavish in spending on her beauty therapies, and Amenla did not want to miss the chance to earn some money after so many days. She could even try her luck in asking the lady for a small loan. Of course, she would have to evade the cops enroute; anyway, since Sushant Lok was at a walking distance, she could do that easily.

She quickly wolfed down a dry slice of bread with some black tea and got ready to leave for Mrs Sethi's house. She locked the door of the room and stepped out. Suddenly, she realised that she had not worn a mask and irritably opened the door again and pulled on a cloth mask on her face.

She rang the bell of Mrs Sethi's house and heard someone shuffling up to the door. Mrs Sethi opened the door and with one look, Amenla sensed that something was not right. The lady looked haggard and sickly and could barely speak.

'Yes, do come in,' she said in a wheezy voice.

Amenla instinctively winced and asked her 'Ma'am are you okay?'

Mrs Sethi broke into a fit of cough and said, 'I'm not well and need help. I think I've got COVID.' Amenla froze in horror and almost turned around and ran. Seeing her face, Mrs Sethi slumped on the ground and looked at Amenla with pleading eyes. 'Please help me. The servant ran away back to her village, and my only son is in the US. He is unable to come as there are no flights,' she said between coughing fits. Seeing that Amenla was still horror stricken and not convinced. She held her hand desperately and said again, 'I have no kith and kin here and will die otherwise. I called you as I could think of no one else. Of course, I will pay you well. I'll give you Rs 2,000 per day.'

The temptation of earning a tidy sum of money clouded her reasoning. In addition to that, Mrs Sethi's offer to pay off the small sum she owed as outstanding rent for her room and her instincts as a former nursing student somehow made Amenla agree to shift into Mrs Sethi's house (which also meant free food and lodging), although she knew that it was a very risky proposition.

Mrs Sethi was very sick, running a high fever and was coughing frantically. Amenla wore two masks and gave her medications which had been prescribed by a doctor over a video consultation. Mrs Sethi's son, too, would be on video call thrice a day, though he seemed more irritated rather than concerned. Three days hence, Amenla was miraculously still okay, but Mrs Sethi's oxygen level began dipping alarmingly. The doctor video consulting Mrs Sethi wanted her to be put immediately on oxygen support. Mrs Sethi's son in the US was trying to arrange a hospital bed for her, but the health system was overwhelmed by April end and all treatment had to be done from home itself. The doctor, sensing that Amenla had some para-medic training, told her to arrange an oxygen cylinder urgently as Mrs Sethi would collapse otherwise.

Amenla surfed the net to find out about oxygen cylinder sellers. She got a WhatsApp forward (a multiple forwarded message) giving a number where one could contact for an oxygen cylinder. She desperately called the number, and a male voice at the other end told her it would cost her Rs. 10,000 and she would have to pick it up from Sikandarpur (another urban village in Gurgaon). Mrs Sethi counted and gave her the money and held her hand in gratitude. Amenla went to Sikandarpur on an e-rickshaw (a few had started plying). She trudged down the filthy lanes of Sikandarpur which looked even more dystopian now, trying to locate the address. She cringed when local loafers catcalled her with obvious racial slurs. 'See, there goes Corona! It is due to these people only that Corona has come to our country.'

She reached the rendezvous point which was a dingy shop. A shallow-looking man took the money from her and gave her a dirty looking and dented cylinder with a regulator and gauge which had seen better days. The equipment looked industrial rather than medical. 'Will this work and is this safe?' she asked. 'Should work. This is all I have; take it or leave it. There are many others who will buy it otherwise,' said the man rather curtly.

Left with no choice, Amenla transported the cylinder back

home. Thankfully, it seemed to work, and Mrs Sethi was put on oxygen support. Mrs Sethi's son came on video call and asked her to show the cylinder. Seeing the condition of the cylinder, he flared up. 'Are you mad and are you trying to cheat my mother? You paid 10K for this unhygienic junk.' Amenla was as it is stressed out and she could not bear it anymore. 'Why don't you come yourself and take care of her? I will leave,' she blurted. Mrs Sethi's son—sensing that if Amenla actually left, there would be no one to take care of Mrs Sethi-immediately calmed down, and instead of apologising, told her that she was doing a fine job and that he was trying to come to India at the earliest.

It was the 6th of May and more than a week since she had moved into Mrs Sethi's house. With all the precautions she was taking and definitely with a lot of good fortune, Amenla was still okay. But Mrs Sethi's health was fluctuating up and down. The oxygen cylinder needed constant filling up. Amenla had found a cylinder filling point just across the road run by a Sikh Charity and had to stand in a queue for over 2 hours before her cylinder was filled each day. She was mentally and physically exhausted. She just wanted the money which Mrs Sethi had promised her and then go back to Nagaland as soon as possible. She pined to see her mother and Joseph.

On 7th May, Mrs Sethi's son informed her that he would be coming down from the US on 10th May on a repatriation flight (Amenla didn't know what that meant). Mrs Sethi seemed visibly happy through the oxygen mask, though her condition had deteriorated over the last few days.

Three days hence, a car stopped outside the house and honked. Amenla peeped outside and found a man getting down from the car, dressed from head to toe in PPE. It was Mrs Sethi's son. He took hesitant steps, reached the door, and entered. He went up to his mother's room without acknowledging Amenla's

'Good morning' and spoke to Mrs Sethi, 'Mom I'm here. I have arranged a hospital bed and we will shift you there tomorrow first thing.' He thereafter rushed out of the house without spending much time and after spraying himself with sanitiser got back into the car and sped away.

That night, Mrs Sethi died. Amenla, too, had developed a mild fever and a cough. What happened after that was a blur; a lot of people came in PPEs and took away Mrs Sethi's body and a flurry of workers busied themselves in sanitising the house. Mrs Sethi's son curtly told Amenla that she could leave. 'Sir, my money which madam had promised me,' she said, amid a bout of cough. He looked at her in horror and disgust. 'Don't come close. Here, take this and just go' and gave a Rs 2,000 note. 'Sir, madam had promised me Rs 2,000 per day. I had taken care of her for 11 days,' protested Amenla. 'Well, Madam is dead now; don't be so greedy. Just take this and get going. I'm not going to give you a rupee more,' he said, throwing another Rs 2,000 note on the table before rushing out of the house. Amenla looked perplexed and was shaken out from her daze when a sanitary worker picked up the note and gave it to her. '*Didi* (sister), this must be yours... we have to seal the house. Please step aside.'

Big, warm tears flowed down her cheeks. Her body was racked with fever and her throat ached as she trudged down the street with her meagre belongings packed in a battered airbag. She passed by the Sikh Charity and the burly Sardar there waved, recognising her. She walked up to the kiosk, and without saying a word, dropped the second 2,000 rupee note which Mrs Sethi's son had thrown at her into the donation box of the charity and walked away.

The e-rickshaw dropped her off in Gurgaon railway station. Amenla bought a ticket and walked through the platform, labouring to breathe. The platform was crowded with a lot of desperate people looking to get back to their villages in the hinterland and smelt of sweat, urine, and utter despondency. She flopped on a bench on Platform 2 and waited for a train which would take her back to the Northeast—at least the air would smell sweeter there.

The Box

@Apoorva Maheshwari

'Anvesha, come here,' called out my dad. As I stood up and walked across the house, I could feel the eyes of the people move with me. That short walk across the white marbled floor of the hall felt like the most difficult steps I had ever taken. As I reached where my father stood, I saw a box in his hand.

'Here, Baba wanted you to have this,' he said as he handed over the box to me. With trembling hands, I took the box and almost instantaneously broke down. The dam of perseverance that had been holding the swift river of tears had finally given way. I had tried too hard to be strong for my family, but now I just couldn't hold it in me anymore.

My dad placed his arm around me and gave a consoling hug. I felt that even he was welling up but the strength of character that I had always admired in him had held back the tears, giving away only a deep breath to display the grief that he was feeling.

As the tears subsided into sniffles, I broke out of the hug and headed to my room. I placed the box on the bed and admired it. It was a beautiful oakwood box. Though it was a little worn out, it still had the regal feel. It was covered with thin, gold-plated sheets that formed elaborate floral patterns. Red and blue jewels adorned the floral pattern in the form of tiny flowers with golden

"

centres. This wasn't the first time I was seeing the box. It had always been placed on the bedside table in my grandparents' room. I had always dreamt of inheriting the box but not the way I just had.

With a deep breath, I finally gathered the courage to open the box. As I threw the lid open, I moved away from it, expecting to be drowned in darkness and sorrow just like Pandora. Instead, I found a piece of paper neatly folded in it. My hands shivered as I picked up the paper. I slowly released the folds to find a message and a pen drive. The message read, 'These are the last few words Baba left for you.' I quickly looked for my laptop and plugged in the pen drive. The window showed a single audio file named, "To my dear Anvi". My eyes were filled with tears as I double-clicked on the file to hear the message. The audio clip played. *My dear Anvi, you might get this box about five to six days after I am gone. Rest assured that I have given proper instructions to Abhishek to sanitise the box so that it is free from the obscure Coronavirus. I really wouldn't want to see you get quarantined because of an old man's parting gift,* chuckled my grandfather.

We have had long debates about your career path in the last six months. I have to admit that they have been the most pleasing sessions of my otherwise monotonous life. Every debate you would come up with reasons of either why you should take up engineering or why becoming a doctor was not your cup of tea. But the question that you asked me a month ago was the most moving. As we lost my dear friend Satish to the Coronavirus, you asked if becoming a doctor was worth it if you lost your life in the line of duty. Did a doctor not have an obligation towards their family and loved ones? Did they not have an obligation towards their children and grandchildren, to guide them and to support them?

Although I tried to explain that the Hippocratic oath was binding on us and formed the basis of the value structure that every doctor followed, you would hear none of it. You were moved by seeing the plight of Satish's family and that was when I was reassured that you had it in you to become a doctor. To be moved by the pain of others, to help others through action or words and to stand up for what you believe is right are the few qualities I would look for in the new trainee doctors before admitting them into the hospital staff.'

You, my child, had all of these qualities and more at such a young age. I can't say that it is because of me and Amma (mother) or your parents that you have developed this sensitivity at such a tender age. The four of us have spent more time with the patients at our hospital then we have with you, but you have never once let us down.

As far as your answer is concerned, I would like to narrate a small episode that recently happened at our hospital. A few weeks back, we had a lady come in. She must have been in her early fifties but due to lack of nutrition looked way older. She walked to the reception and asked to meet me. As I was on my rounds, she was asked to wait in the lobby.

It so happened that I had just reached the lobby to find the woman handing over her only gold bangle to the woman sitting next to her. The woman refused to take the bangle, but the old lady insisted.

'I have no one in my family. If I can help you and your husband, I will feel like I have helped my daughter and her family. Please don't say no, please take it,' said the old lady as she handed over the bangle to the woman.

I reached out to our receptionist, and he informed me that the old lady wanted to meet me. I asked him to send her in and went to my cabin. Soon, there was a soft knock on the door and the lady peeked through the open door with a smile. She asked if she could come in.

She sat down on the stool across the table. She then pulled out her sanitiser bottle and a pair of gloves. I was amazed at the hygiene standards that she was following. She then removed a packet from her bag.

She held it in her hand and said, 'These are some masks that I would like to give you. Some of my friends and I have stitched them. We have taken utmost care that these masks remain sanitised and free of any contaminants. We have donated these masks to several clinics so that they can be distributed free of cost to any person who needs them.'

I was touched by her gesture and agreed to take them in. I asked her how many masks she had donated this way. She said that her group had made more than five thousand masks. They worked for four to five hours every day relentlessly through the four-month lockdown, making about twenty to twenty-five masks daily.

My next question was definitely how she had the resources to do so. She smiled and said that she was a widow. From the pension she received, she funded her charity work. She said she had no children of her own and no real family, so she decided to make the whole city her family.

She placed the packet in the tray and got up to leave. As she did so, I tried to offer her some money in return for the masks. She said that she had enough and didn't need the money. It was only then when I told her to consider it as a tiny help to buy more cloth for the next batch of masks that she finally agreed.

I opened the door for her and watched as she walked out. The young woman who had been sitting on the bench promptly got up and rushed to the lady. She touched her feet and sought her blessings.

The lady gave her blessings with her hands slightly above the head of the young women to ensure that she didn't make contact. As the young woman rose, the lady asked the young woman to show her hands. The lady squeezed some sanitiser from the bottle on to the young woman's palms and reprimanded her for not maintaining social distancing. She then sweetly smiled and left.

People like her, Anvi, are the jewels of our society. These acts of selflessness are what keeps society strong and healthy. When people like her who have little to give take steps like these, it motivates us to be better humans. What Satish did might have cost him his life, but I am sure he died with the satisfaction of having helped so many people. As I, too, sit here on this bed, pondering over my work during this period, I hope it will make you see our commitment to our jobs in a better light.' A bittersweet tear trinkled down my cheeks.

I love you, my dear child, and wish you all the best for your future endeavours. Have a great life ahead and remember that I will always be there watching over you if not in my physical form but definitely as a star. Make sure to look out for me at night, within the profligate depths of the vast sky.

There was a small laugh, and the audio clip came to an end. Anvesha smiled even though her face was covered with streams of tears. She ejected the pen drive and placed it into the box. Just as she was about to put it back, she felt her fingers touch a velvet cloth. She felt that something was wrapped with the cloth. She slowly peered through the layers to find a stethoscope. It was the same stethoscope that her grandfather had used for several years of his practice. The one Anvesha had wanted as a child. She had even gotten her grandfather to buy another stethoscope as she had claimed this one as hers. She hugged the stethoscope as once again tears rolled down her cheeks.

She carefully kept the stethoscope in the velvet cloth and placed the pen drive and the letter back into the box. She wiped the tears from her face and went to the washroom to splash some cold water. As she padded her face dry, she looked for the number of her coaching class.

As the receptionist picked up the phone, Anvesha said, 'Hi, I am Anvesha Mishra. I am a student of the Enthuse batch for JEE. I would like to change my course to NEET. Could you please tell me about the procedure for that?' The receptionist asked Anvesha to hold the line as she got her the details. Anvesha readily accepted as a soft smile made its way on her face.

Soaring High

@Sanam Vaseem Shaikh

Never-ending period of lockdown it had seemed
People feared never to meet again,
Everywhere there was just a sigh!

Am I the one to sit and regret?
It's not time to sob over things,
It's time to rejuvenate your being
Get up and let the spirit spark.

Boost your soul, learn a new role
I made a choice to console,
By writing the content close to my emotions
I penned and got published.

I gained a new enthusiasm, I lost the old soul
Now I'm a new me, don't fear the others,
People try to pull
The Almighty holds me high, and I fly, and I fly!

Pause To Live

@Vivek Gulati

'Good afternoon, everyone, thank you for gracing this occasion wherein we showcase our budding authors and their books. May I introduce my very good friend and author, Shubham Singh? He will be reading excerpts from his book, Pause to Live.'

So, Nivedita Basu held up my book for all to see and gestured towards me to come to the mic. This was the moment I had been dreading all along, I had even requested her—who is my school mate too, to do the honours. We were at a bookstore famous for holding book release functions, and today was my-dream-come-true moment. I had never ever thought that I would one day be releasing my own book here. An avid reader, I had till now entered the portals of this reputed store to only buy books of my favourite authors—all this looked and felt surreal. From having written the book under her guidance to signing it for a few buyers, it had been quite a transition for a person like me who had graduated from being an ardent reader to a published author. Sharing the stage with the ever young and beautiful Nivedita (you guessed it, I am biased!) whose writing had been an influencing factor in my turning towards penning my thoughts, was too overwhelming a moment for me to register. To be even sharing the dais with Nivedita Basu, whose books sold like hot cakes and the last one still topping the charts, was another item checked off my bucket list.

Anyway, more of that later. Let me begin:

'Hello, dear audience. Thank you for taking the time out to listen to me. I am truly honoured. This is my debut in the world of writing and standing here in front of all of you and amongst some finest writers is still taking time to sink in,' I smiled—a tad nervously, and Nivedita reading into it, egged the audience to join her in clapping. Bless her.

This gave me the confidence I needed and relaxed my grip on the mic. 'So now that I have been trapped by my editor and a wonderful friend, I will do the book reading but in a unique style. I will take you through the journey via a bypass, which will give you the overview of the book in a crisp manner and hopefully not bore you,' I smiled.

'For the sake of clarity, the book has been divided in three eras, namely, BC, C19, AC. To elaborate, life before Covid (BC), during Covid (C19), and after Covid (AC). Through my story, I have basically tried to portray that with positivity, one can survive amidst the most perpetual of agonies and sense of desolation.'

I could feel the audience stirring, sitting up straight. Their body language changed and so did mine and my tone was also more confident now and relaxed.

Phase 1—BC

Life was good, business was booming, and my world was all rosy. I was happy writing headlines and body copy for advertisements. By contributing substantially to my clients' marketing strategy, I not only gained their respect but also witnessed huge growth in my company's turnover. On the personal front, I couldn't devote much time to our family, but full credit goes to my better half for taking control and raising our son to be a responsible and caring young man. Her support provided me the fuel to channelise all my energies in accelerating the growth chart of my fledging Advertising agency.

My team was growing, and as I started delegating work, I found time hanging on my hands. In the world of advertising, getting a revert from the client is a hard task, as some of you must be aware. To keep my creative juices flowing, I started writing, first blogs and then short stories. I am a Forest Officer's son, and my childhood has been most unusual (privileges of growing close to nature, read: jungle). I had shared my life experiences casually with friends and family till now. They reacted positively and that gave me a further boost. One particular school friend very critically evaluated my work and showed me how it could be further improved. This person was nobody else than my Editor, Nivedita. Like a typical male chauvinist, I immediately thought that she was just being arrogant and was only trying to be negative to put me down. Everyone else had been so positive about my work till then. Upset, I discussed it with a common friend, who told me to stop being prejudiced and recognise good advice when you see it. Nivedita was a very proficient writer and had been published many times over. She had written novels, too. It was at that moment that I realised she was genuinely helping me to write better.

Sheepishly, I called her and apologised for my reaction to her critical evaluation of my work. Nivedita laughed it off, saying, 'I have known you from school days, and so, was expecting this reaction, no worries.' After that, we really connected and started sharing our work with each other. While she continued to fine tune my work, what really amused and motivated me was her acceptance of my need to write and better it.

Phase 2—C 19

After Prime Minister's announcement that the nation would be observing a token lockdown, it hit upon us suddenly that the pandemic had reached our doorsteps. The lockdown expectedly got extended, days turned into months and all the businesses, offices and educational institutions were closed down. Being confined to our houses, the initial reaction from everyone was: 'Loving it, spending quality time with family finally,' 'finding myself,' and 'learning new hobbies'; all positive thoughts and happiness all around. So far so good. Slowly, it dawned on all of us that this was it. There was no immediate end in sight. The party had ended abruptly. Despair flooded all around. This was the new normal. WFH (work from home) was the go-to mantra. When businesses feel the pinch, advertising sector is the first to be hit. For months with zero business, one had to take desperate measures to survive. I had to harden myself to take the toughest decision of my life, asking quite a few of my team members to leave. We tried to compensate them to the best of our ability, but this decision had a major effect on my psychology. Soon, the pandemic drew even more close. A few members of our extended family, friends and associates were snatched away from us by the horrific claws of C19. Financial worries, sombre atmosphere, and idle mind made a powerful cocktail which affected me adversely; while life had been all rosy BC, now it was all shades of greys and blacks.

After my family got affected by C19 and fortunately survived, I thought that if this pandemic has proved anything, it is that "There is no tomorrow." One has to live for today. The rat race is endless and now we knew that it may not always have a happy ending. By postponing your bucket list, you not only lose the precious today and the future can be just snatched away at any moment.

So C19 gave me like all of us an opportunity to pause and plan the AC in a manner that we live the present, properly and joyfully. Do today all that you have planned for tomorrow. Meet relatives, friends, visit places, pay your respects, say your apologies, acknowledge your love, hug whom you have always wanted to and do all of this today. No planning or postponing for an unknown tomorrow.

Phase 3—AC

From 18 hours a day, 6 days a week; I decided that 'enough is enough'; now, I would live at my pace and take it easy, and I would only take selective assignments that sufficed the mind more than the wallet, meet all those people I had always wanted to but had never found the time. As Covid restrictions opened, I, too, re-visited my bucket list. I had always wanted to see Ladakh. Its beautiful landscape and panoramic views had remained with me since the movie "3 Idiots", and so, off we went there and got the first check on the list. God in his profound wisdom had given me the opportunity to pause, reflect and analyse in the guise of a pandemic and I decided I wanted to get lighter, not only physically but by also letting go of my inhibitions, my self-created emotional burdens. I wanted to start living the moment, to put it succinctly.

One of the first things that was to take up writing again, this time *'dil se'* (from the heart) and devote some serious time to it. I never wanted to live in regret now, never wanted to have this feeling of 'if only I had', ever. I broached the topics which I had not touched before—topics close to my heart, wrote tributes to my parents, and tried to convey all that I could not communicate while they were around. Nivedita found that my writing in the AC phase had become more refined, mature, and carried a depth that it had earlier lacked. It had to be—finally, I was writing what

I had always felt but was hesitant to express. The best compliment I received was when she called me up one day to say, 'Now, your writing reflects what I thought was missing—empathy and sentiments mixed with cerebral.' In layman's terms, a better mix of brain and heart, while earlier it was just heart. To me, those were golden words. It spurred me to write more and explore my creativity. Meanwhile, Nivedita referred me to few websites where you can send your work to get published online. Readers' reviews and ratings help to encourage and to self-introspect. My very first poem—a tribute to my late mother (to whom, like all of us, I owe everything) got very appreciative comments from the readers which kickstarted my journey as a serious writer.

My friend, philosopher, and guide—Nivedita—again came to my rescue. She, being an editor with a few major publishing houses, asked me to start contributing to various anthologies that these publishing houses were introducing time to time. This started my new journey, and my dream of seeing my work in a printed book came true. Money started trickling in with few books doing exceedingly well as they had lot of promising writers, who were much better and experienced than me. There was marked improvement in my output after I went through the works of eminent writers as each had their own way of presenting the narrative.

Just few months back, I bounced off a story idea to Nivedita on how different people have survived the pandemic and how their lives have changed post C19. Some have unfortunately gone downhill as they couldn't fight for survival due to mental health issues, but there are people like me who developed new interests, found a guide, and survived. Nivedita got equally excited and said, 'That's just brilliant; just go ahead and manifest this into a book. It will be so inspirational for others, on how to come out of difficult situations. I promise you that I will edit your book and not charge a penny.'

So, friends, here I am in front of you with "Pause to Live", wishing that it raises hope within people especially in times of despair. But my biggest achievement through this book will be if it is able to imbibe a feeling in you all that we should take a pause in our normal lives also, analyse and reflect and accordingly alter the path of our lives or slow down the speed of our lives which may enable us to live our today with the respect that it deserves.

I also pray that you, my dear audience, find an angel to guide you through the dark phases, like I got in Nivedita. I would like to take this opportunity to thank her for all her guidance and the encouragement she gave whenever I had doubts or faltered. Thank you, Nivedita, for being my lighthouse and seeing me safely ashore. I know I have troubled you at the most inopportune time of the day, but your gentle words and immense patience has today borne fruit. Dear friends, my journey through the pandemic proves the saying, 'Every cloud has a silver lining.' I take this opportunity to request our esteemed publishers to deduct 10% from my share of royalty and donate it to institutions dealing with mental health issues.

Thanks a ton, Nivedita, for making me what I am today, and I hope my friends, you, too, find your Nivedita just as I did mine.

Taking a deep breath and smiling at Nivedita, I opened my book to read out a few hard-hitting paragraphs about my fight during the pandemic.

A Forlorn Land

@Arun Hariharan

The tired wayfarer trudged the bleak land,
The effervescent chaos called life seemed bygone,
Man's proudest creations stood bedecked in sand,
All their allure and grandeur lay pitiably shorn.
Where has all of perfidious mankind disappeared?
Where are all the poison miasma belching monsters?
'Oh, traveller,' blared a loudspeaker… 'Have you not heard?'
Of the vile pestilence, ravaging the last many summers.
Workplaces were desolate, homes were hungry,
As people gasped for breath in hopeless stupor,
and the forsaken Gods seemed relentlessly angry,
Pleaded a battered humanity, 'How much more?'
They just looked down from above and smirked
'Reap now, you repine man, for my creations you ne'er valued!'

And Then He Became a Man

@Vasudha Kapoor Duggal

Kallu quickly jumped out of his *charpoy* (roped wooden bed) and ran down the *gully* (lane) to the common bathroom area. He had woken up late and needed to join his online classes. If there was anything he enjoyed the most, it was school and studying. Now in class eight, he had consistently been one of the class toppers in the local Mumbai government school. He was often at the receiving end of his friends' jokes for being so focused in academics while they pursued other interests.

It took Kallu exactly ten minutes to freshen up. He came back to his *jhuggi* (hut) and lovingly took out his smartphone to log in to his class. It was the most precious gift he had ever got, thanks to his father's employer, who always enquired about the family's well-being. His father, Govindram, worked as a peon in a Seth's office. When lockdown was imposed in March 2020 and schools closed, studies came to a grinding halt for a while. After about two months, classes resumed in the online mode and hence many in his Dharavi settlement missed out these classes. Not many had computers or smartphones. But after a casual chat with Govindram, the Sethji gave him his old smartphone so that the bright Kallu could continue studying.

Kallu, of course, was on cloud nine with his prized possession. Few kids of his age owned a smartphone in the Dharavi *basti* (locality). From attending classes to playing some interesting online games to watching shows and movies, he also was the proud owner of an email account. Apart from playing weekend cricket with them, he rarely joined his friends to play cards or in their regular *sutta* (smoking) sessions.

Life was good for Kallu. His mother ran a tea stall for a few hours in the afternoon, very close to Dharavi, outside the gates of a large factory area. Between the seven to eight thousand rupees that she made and the fifteen thousand rupees salary his father got, they managed their *jhuggi* rent and day-to-day sustenance. His eight-year-old sister and six-year-old brother were engrossed playing between themselves along with other *jhuggi* children.

Kallu was busy with his online classes and studies and all the other interests his smartphone provided him. Someday, he dreamed, he would become a *sarkari afsar* (government officer) after completing his studies. He would take those competitive exams and fulfil his dreams. A good salary would enable him to take care of his family and maybe build a *pucca* (cemented) house for themselves.

Weekends were all about cricket with his friends right through the day. His best friend, Binay, was a very good bowler and Kallu loved to bat at his balls. He had never amassed more than 70 runs against Binay's bowling much as he aspired to make a century. The *paanwala uncle ji* (neighbourhood betelnut stall owner) promised him 250 rupees if he ever made a century, but despite this incentive, he never made it. This caused much anxiety, and he pondered why, with all the practice, he did not make it.

One Sunday, he stepped out determined to score a hundred.

Today I have to score a century. I must get those 250 rupees. Today, I will chant Ganpati Bappa Morya (Hail Lord Ganesh) right through my batting.

The game started and he scored 50 runs easily, like always. The challenge always started after that. One couldn't say whether it was fatigue or loss of focus that used to spoil his game. But on that Sunday, he took extra-long breaks two to three times to regain his energy and did not stop remembering *Ganpati Bappa Morya.* With sturdy determination, he continued batting till he was just 8 runs short.

He looked up at the sky and then faced Binay. And there he went, hitting a sixer! As everyone clapped and cheered, the paanwala uncle flashed 250 rupees at Kallu. *'Kallu, bus do run aur le le bacchhe* (Kallu, make two runs more, son).' Kallu looked at him and smiled happily. For the next 7 balls, he did not score any runs.

'Ganpati Bappa Morya,' he said aloud as he flung the next ball far outside the designated boundary. Finally! He had done it! He jumped with joy and ran to hug Binay. Happily pocketing the 250 rupees, he ran to his *jhuggi* to share his feat with his father.

Kallu recalled his reward in the previous *Ganpati* celebrations, where he had participated in the local cultural festival along with his friends. Under the tutelage of Mahant *Bhaiya* (elder brother), they had put up an interesting hour-long play for which they had fun-filled practice sessions for an entire month. Kallu played the role of a cranky old man and his quirks and funny dialogues had evoked a lot of laughter and appreciation. That time, too, the *paanwala* uncle had given him and two other performers hundred rupees each as their reward. Mahant *Bhaiya* hugged them all and told them to participate the following year too. Kallu had discovered another skill of his and there on, often mimicked film dialogues in front of the mirror and his family. So, between his studies, smartphone, cricket and mimicry, Kallu led quite a contented life.

However, life was different outside his little world. Covid had spread its tentacles all over the world, limiting all activities. Unfortunate and sad stories made the rounds every day. Newspapers had little else to write about except Covid-related news. The closest that Covid came to Kallu was when in December 2020, his grandfather contracted it. Fortunately, he recovered. And everyone prayed for the new year to bring better times for everyone.

By February and March 2021, it almost seemed as if Covid was dying out and heralded the arrival of normal times until one evening in April, Govindram returned home with a body ache and slight fever. The next day, the fever increased, and he had lost sense of taste and smell. Two days later, Kallu's mother, too, lost her sense of taste and smell. The two were confined to their *jhuggi* while Kallu and his siblings were sent to their uncle's *jhuggi* a hundred metres away. As their condition worsened, his mother could no longer cook, and food was sent by the uncle and neighbours. Many cases had suddenly erupted in their cluster. There was mayhem all around.

Twice, Kallu took his father for CT scans at the local government healthcare centre in his uncle's rickshaw. He was running around for medicines as quite a few were not available. All hell broke loose when the doctor proclaimed his father's condition to be critical as his oxygen level had fallen very low. He needed to be hospitalised. Kallu rushed him to the government civil hospital, but there was no one to attend to him. Amidst the crowd and frenzy there, doctors and nurses were nowhere to be seen. Kallu pleaded with the staff to get someone to attend to his father. After about three hours, his father was put on an oxygen cylinder while lying on the floor in the huge reception. Kallu was alone with his father as his uncle stayed away, lest he got infected. For three days, with mask and gloves on, Kallu was by his father's side, tending to him and trying to get the doctors and nurses to attend to him. There were no beds available, and many patients were lying on the floor even in the corridors.

All around were anxious people attending to their loved ones. Amidst much wailing and crying, Kallu witnessed five deaths during his stay there. This unprecedented kind of crisis was something people had never witnessed before. As his father's condition refused to improve, Kallu resorted to praying. He found it hard to control his tears as he saw his father lying in a semi-conscious state. Never had he seen his father so weak and helpless. When he was slightly better, three days later, he made Kallu promise, '*Kha meri kasam, Kallu. Tu bada afsar banega aur agar mujhe kuch ho gaya, toh tu maa aur bachcha log ka dhyan rakhe ga* (Promise me Kallu, you will grow up to be big officer and if anything happens to me, you will look after your mother and your siblings).'

Kallu was pretty upbeat then. '*Kuch nahin hoga baba tumhe. Jaldi theek ho jaaoge* (Don't worry, father, nothing will happen to you, you will recover).'

So much had changed in the next few days. Baba's condition had consistently deteriorated, so much so that now even Kallu was losing hope. The scenario around was further dampening his spirit.

He answered the frequent calls from his mother and uncle, constantly updating them. It was over two weeks that he hadn't attended any classes. He barely left his father, just rushing home once or twice each day to freshen up and get food.

One unfortunate day, at about 5 a.m., Kallu woke with a start as someone was nudging him to get up. He saw it was the middle-aged woman who had come with her husband ever since he came to the hospital. She woke him and made frantic gestures, pointing to his father. One look at his father and it didn't take long for Kallu to realise what she was saying. He sprang up and went towards his father and shook him, '*Baba, baba... utho, Baba.* (Get up, father).' But to no avail. His father was no longer breathing. Kallu ran, calling out to the staff behind the counter. They looked at his father and nodded sympathetically.

From then on, Kallu's life changed. Gone were those carefree days. For weeks, the family just sat in a daze, numbed by grief. Kallu felt like a grown man with the weight of the responsibilities that had befallen him. Instead of studies, he was now worried about making a living.

After about a fortnight, Kallu's mother resumed her tea stall business. She had to earn; she had to feed everyone. Kallu started accompanying her not just for moral support but to help. His mother used to sell tea from 11 a.m. to about 4 p.m. On his uncle's advice, they added chips, biscuits, *paan parag* and *gutka* (tobacco) to their sale offerings. This got them more customers. For a month, Kallu missed his studies as he helped run the stall with his mother. But it made him miserable. Studies were important. He had promised his father to become an *afsar*.

Until an idea struck him. *Why not keep the stall open till late evening? Why not attend classes in the mornings and manage the stall in the evenings? His mother could go home at her usual time while he manned it in the evening. This way, he could continue his studies and also make that extra buck through the extended stall timings.*

Pleased, he proposed this idea to his mother and uncle. Though his mother was reluctant, his uncle immediately gave him the go-ahead and managed to convince his mom. And thus started the new phase of his life. Attending online classes during the day and managing the tea stall in the evenings covered up for his father's earnings to some extent. On Sundays, he continued with his cricket and then managed the stall.

Kallu often pondered upon the tragedy that had befallen him. Why had his world changed so suddenly? Why? However, he conceded he was not alone. The second Covid wave had spelled misery and doom in many homes. Almost everyone he knew had been affected in some way or the other. Kallu was fortunate; his father's employer had sent twenty-five thousand rupees after his father's demise and had even offered Kallu a job. But then, the Sethji himself had suggested that Kallu finish his studies and thereafter think of a full-time job.

'Kallu, Kallu, aree zara chote ko sambhaal. Roti nahin banane de raha! (Kallu, please look after your young brother, he is not allowing me to cook!)' called out his mother. Kallu kept his smartphone aside and got up to attend to his mother's call. With Baba around, he never had to bother about his siblings or any housework. But now he was in his father's shoes. He could not ignore it. Life had changed.

Transcendent-Virus

@Monika Patel

Never heard before words like pandemic, quarantine, social distancing, PPE kit, WFH.

Never experienced before lack of planes, trains, buses, and taxis.

Never stood before in long queues to fetch daily essentials.

Never used before, sanitisers, masks, gloves and shields to stay safe.

Never lived before in self-isolation to keep family and society safe.

****

Never seen before sights of deserted roads, empty public places, unoccupied educational institutions, and vacant office buildings.

Never seen before the poor man walking all the way to his far away home.

Never seen before the medics in such distress and anguish struggling to save lives.

Never seen before the overburdened staff at hospitals working day and night till they fell from exhaustion.

Never seen before families forced to leave their infected loved ones at isolation centres to be quarantined, only hoping to be united with them soon.

Never seen before the struggle of loved ones to get prescribed medications and oxygen.

Never seen before the getting together of like-minded folks to help feed the needy and strays.

Never seen before the dedication of the police and civic officials working day and night streamlining the situation.

Never seen before the rush to develop a vaccine to save the human race.

Never seen before the empathy of a person for another.

****

This once-in-a-century event taught us to respect our doctors, medical staff, epidemiologists.

To care for and respect our essential needs suppliers, sanitary workers, delivery people, law enforcement personnel.

To be healthy in mind and body, to take care of oneself is not a self-indulgence.

To use our resources prudently and to save for any future needs.

To be tech savvy, to work from wherever you are and to value the job.

To be able to live for today, stay in touch with family and friends and respect life.

This transcendent virus taught us empathy, resilience, and dignity for life. It has made us aware of the disparities that our society is dealing with. Let us all acknowledge the learnings and practice them to be better prepared for future emergencies and for generations to come.

With You, For You

@Apurva Tandon

Mamta groaned as she tried to reach out for her phone. The headache was back again, worse this time. And the stupid body ache also refused to go. It had been two weeks now and she shuddered at the thought of having contracted that dreaded virus everyone was talking about. She had been putting it down to her delayed menopause, but now, she thought—maybe she needed to call Dr Joshi.

The phone stopped ringing as she picked it up. It was Akshat. Her dutiful, loving son, calling up to check on his parents. The mother in her beamed as she started typing out a message to him. Ever since the PM had announced the lockdown, he had been calling every day. She had tried convincing him that they were fine, and he should concentrate on his studies. After all, not everyone gets admission into ESMT, Berlin, that too on full scholarship. She sent the message and shuffled to find a comfortable spot on her favourite couch. She wanted to make the most of this quiet. The lockdown had its advantages, especially because their apartment building was bang on the main road and traffic noise was unrelenting. Mamta was determined to enjoy her peace, at least till Alok came back from his card game. Something inside of her cringed at the thought of Alok. Alok Kumar, the prized catch with his cushy-bank job. Alok Kumar, at the altar where her burning desire to study further was sacrificed by her grateful parents. And she, the eldest of the three sisters, was compliant to this life term.

'Didi (sister), should I make tea?' Obaida's loud call woke her up from her reverie. 'Yes, please!' she shouted back as she saw the time. It was already past 6 p.m. Alok would be back soon and she had not even started writing her blog today.

Her blog! *'Ghar Ghar ki Kahaniyan'* (Stories of different homes) It was the best gift Akshat had ever given her. Her sensitive son had recognised her spark of storytelling and had tutored her to use the computer and start a blog. What started as a hobby had now become her lifeline. The comments of her readers kept her going and made her feel a little less useless every day. But today her readers will have to wait. Alok should be back any minute. He had no interest in her blog. Actually, after his retirement, he had no interest in anything, other than the daily Bridge session with his buddies. And since all his friends lived in the same building, the bridge sessions were on—lockdown be damned!

'Didi, chai! (Sister, tea!)' So, saying, Obaida plonked herself on the ground. 'Arre, (Hey) you are not writing today? What will your millions of admirers do for entertainment?' Obaida giggled. Mamta looked at Obaida indulgently. One of the main reasons Mamta could spend time on her blogs was Obaida, her full-time help who had been with them for the last three years. She had come highly recommended by her previous employer Arora Aunty, a pleasant lady living across the road, who had gone abroad with her husband to live with their son who was in the Indian Foreign Service.

Obaida had taken over all the household responsibilities and, even though 6 years younger to Mamta, Obaida was like an older sister to her, pampering and looking after all her needs. Mamta, on her part, couldn't imagine life without Obaida's care and help. As the two women sat sipping their tea on that balcony, neither of them had an inkling of what tomorrow had in store for them.

'Didi, Didi get up! Please!' Mamta woke up with a startle. Alok had already rushed to the bedroom door. 'What happened?' Mamta asked as she saw Obaida's tear stained face. *'Didi Alam ko bacha lo.* (Please save Alam)' 'Oh, him again,' muttered Alok as he walked out of the room.

Alam, Obaida's only son from a failed marriage, was living and working in a factory in Mumbai. He was an honest young man, working hard to be able to look after his mother. Between her sobs Obaida explained that a friend of Alam's had called Obaida. Alam's factory had been shut down without any notice or compensation. And when confronted by the workers, the owners had unleashed goons upon them. Alam was one of the workers who was beaten mercilessly and was now battling for his life. No big hospital was taking him in and the doctor in their slum was helpless without proper facilities.

Mamta's mind went blank. Her heart ached for Obaida. Alok! He had friends in high places, he had friends in Mumbai! He can help. She held Obaida's hand and rushed to the balcony. Not once did Alok look up while Obaida narrated the incident to him. Then he looked up and said coldly, 'Send some money. I can't go tapping my resources for random people.' 'Random people? He is Obaida's son, Alok. Our Obaida.' Alok put his newspaper down and said, 'This is not a blog Mamta. This is real life. It could already be a police case. I am not getting involved.'

Mamta felt Obaida quietly take her hands out of Mamta's grip. 'Let it be Didi. I will manage. *Allah meherban hoga* (God will help).'

Mamta was shaken up! Obaida's helplessness became her own, she could not bear to sit back and do nothing. But what?

She knew nobody in Mumbai. She imagined herself in Obaida's shoes and almost fainted just thinking about a situation like this with Akshat in another city all alone and hurt. Almost as if on cue, her mobile rang. It was Akshat!! Her heart sank. It was 3 a.m. in Berlin, why was Akshat calling. Her phone stopped ringing abruptly and she could hear Alok's phone ringing. She rushed to the balcony. Alok was clutching the newspaper tightly and repeatedly shouting into the phone, 'Don't worry, I will do something. I will do everything. Nothing will happen to you.' Mamta sank into the nearest chair. 'What happened to Akshat?' Before Alok could reply, Obaida burst into the balcony and almost screamed, 'Didi, Alam is sinking. The doctor has asked him to be moved right now to a big hospital. No hospital is ready to admit him. Please help him. He will die.'

'To hell with Alam,' Alok screamed, 'My son is stuck in a foreign country with a red alert of COVID and he has been asked to vacate the accommodation with no place to go and you want me to worry about Alam? Just get me Akshat's passport number from the brown diary and get lost from here, both of you, I need to think. Akshat is all alone.'

As if in a trance, Mamta handed the diary over to Alok. She stood there while Alok called people after people, repeatedly giving Akhat's passport number to and saying, 'I will remain indebted to you for life, please do something.'

Mamta needed a cup of tea, or aspirin or something to drown the overwhelming tsunami that was whirling inside her brain. She came to the kitchen and saw Obaida chopping vegetables while relentless tears kept flowing down her face. Mamta was overwhelmed with emotions for this selfless and brave woman, who could lose her only hope in life but was going about with her chores because it had to be done.

On an impulse. Mamta hugged Obaida and said, 'I am so sorry I am not able to help you.' The two women held each other and both of them cried over the two young men in far off lands needing urgent help. Then Obaida held her shoulder and said, 'Don't worry about Akshat baba. Let me talk to Arora madam.' Mamta was stunned that in her acute sorrow also Obaida was thinking about helping her.

Wrenching herself from Obaida's arms, Mamta rushed to her room. Her laptop lay open and beckoning. On an impulse she went to her blog site. There were messages from her readers wondering where her daily story was. Some force took over Mamta. She started pouring her heart out. About Obaida, about Alok, about Akshat, about Alam, about her helplessness. Exhausted and empty of all emotions, she stared blankly at the screen after posting the story. And then it happened! Her readers started responding. Before her eyes, a chain was formed, strings were pulled, and Alam was reached. He was being shifted to a renowned hospital in Worli. Mamta was stupefied. She, the helpless, useless Mamta had done it—Alam would be saved! She had to put Obaida out of her misery. She snapped her laptop shut and rushed out of the room, almost colliding with Obaida.

'Didi! Arora aunty can't help me, but her son's close friend is responsible for helping Indian students get out of foreign countries. Quickly give me Akshat baba's passport number and phone number. He will be safe.' Obaida's eyes were shining.

Mamta hugged her and screamed, 'Alam is safe. My readers have arranged for him to go to a hospital. Our prayers have been answered Obaida.'

Mamta remembered something that her father used to tell her as a child 'God is always closer to you than you think he is.'

From his room Alok watched the two happy, selfless souls laugh as they held each other and went round and round the room.

The Flight Back Home

@ Arun Hariharan

'So then, as we have opportunity, let us do good to everyone.'
—*Galatians 6:10*

It was an hour since the Air India Boeing 777 made a touchdown in the San Francisco Airport. The aircraft had been vacated and the crew stood on the tarmac while a PPE clad maintenance crew fumigated and sanitised the plane. In normal times, the crew would have gone to the terminal and taken a break and refreshed by the time the aircraft was being readied for the return flight. But this time it was different. The flight crew too was in PPE as they boarded back the aircraft once the maintenance crew gave a thumbs-up sign.

Kabeer sat in the cockpit munching a Snickers and sipping some coconut water, trying to soak up calories for the long flight back to Mumbai. He could see on his screen - the passengers, all clad in PPE slowly board the flight to gingerly take their seats one by one.

Not that the ex-Airforce Veteran Wing Commander Kabeer Ahmed had not been in VUCA (volatility, uncertainty, complexity, and ambiguity) situations before. In fact, he had been awarded the Vir Chakra, India's third highest gallantry award during the Kargil War.

But today was different. Dealing with soldiers in war-like situations was something else. Here they were all civilians—old folks, women, children, this VUCA was also very different. Since his retirement from the IAF in 2010, he had been flying for Air India for a decade now and was due to retire from here too, towards the end of the year—on 30th Nov 2020 to be precise. The COVID situation was unprecedented anywhere in the world and Air India had started flying its *"Vande Bharat"* or repatriation flights to get back Indians stuck in foreign lands due to the suspension of all air travel due to the pandemic starting 7th May 2020. This flight was the first one out of the US—from San Francisco to Mumbai.

His chain of thoughts was broken when the head flight purser, Damayanti Mishra knocked at the cockpit door and informed him that all passengers had boarded, and they were ready to go. Ahmed smiled and nodded back to her and turned and spoke to Ravish, his co-pilot, 'So, shall we get going then?' Ravish gave a thumbs up signal as they switched on the engines and the turbines began whining.

Soon the jet liner was on the taxiway with its large twin engines roaring and once the ATC gave the go-ahead, took off uneventfully on the long journey over the Pacific and Indian Oceans back to India.

'This is your Captain, Kabeer Ahmed. Welcome to Air India Vande Bharat Flight No. AI 174 from San Francisco to Mumbai. Our journey will take all of twenty-one hours and let me assure you that you have the finest crew of Air India serving you to make your journey safe and comfortable. Hope all of you are keeping fine. I know these are unprecedented times and we are indeed privileged to be able facilitate you to get back to your loved ones. Enjoy the flight. Jai Hind!'

It was a long and boring flight, largely over the Pacific. They were about three and a half hours in flight now and cruising smoothly. There was a knock at the cockpit door, it was Damayanti. She looked a little flustered and blurted 'Captain, we need help. We have a situation on the flight, with the passenger in Seat 23B to be precise.' Kabeer took the manifest from Damayanti and scrolled down the passenger names, the passenger on seat 23B was Murtaza Hassan, Male, 55. Kabeer gestured to Ravish to man the cockpit and accompanied Damayanti down the aisle.

There indeed was a commotion. About four passengers were having a heated argument with the passenger on Seat 23B and an Air Hostess who was unsuccessfully trying to calm the frayed nerves.

'Hello gentlemen! Calm down. I'm the Captain here, this is no way to behave, and you are all endangering this flight,' said Kabeer crisply. 'We are not endangering this flight, he is,' said the fat lady passenger on Seat 23C accusingly. 'First, he takes off his mask and coughs and now he's saying something which sounded Arabic and very suspicious. We must search him and hold him in custody, I feel he's some kind of a terrorist,' added the Sikh.

'Nobody will do any such thing and Mr Hassan, what were you saying?' asked Kabeer. 'I'm acutely asthmatic and I find it a problem to wear the mask for long. I am flying to India as my mother is on her death bed, so I was just saying a small prayer to ease her suffering and I'm no terrorist, you can search me if you want to,' said Hassan in a scared voice, unable to control the tears tumbling out of his eyes. 'All these Muslims are the same; don't trust them, Captain. Please have this man restrained,' shouted another passenger.

Kabeer could take no more of it. 'For your kind information I am a Muslim, too, and I'm flying you all back home. Do you also know that I was in the Indian Air Force before this, and I am a Vir Chakra awardee? I will tolerate no more of this rabble and order you all to go back to your seats or else I will be forced to land at the nearest airport and hand you all over to the cops for putting this flight at risk,' he said curtly. The passengers reluctantly slunk back to their seats with a sheepish look on their face, muttering to themselves.

'Damayanti, why don't you shift Mr Hassan to the front row reserved for crew? I think one seat is vacant, that way no one would have an issue,' said Kabeer. Hassan looked visibly relieved and mumbled a thank you to Kabeer clutching his hand.

****

Kabeer was running a mild fever and Ayesha, his 21-year-old daughter was at the back seat of his car as he sped through the empty streets of Delhi from their house in Defence Colony to the Army Base Hospital in Delhi Cantonment. Ayesha had a small oxygen cylinder strapped on with a respirator fitted on her face through which she was noisily breathing. It was late in the night and by the time they reached near the Base Hospital, Kabeer spotted a long line of cars stretching right up to Baird Place, almost a mile from the Hospital gate. A few harried looking Military Police personnel were trying to restore some order.

Kabeer got down to find out what exactly was happening. The nearest MP Sergeant told him that there were a lot of people ahead of him waiting for admission at the BH and for now the hospital was screening and admitting only the sickest of patients as they had run out of beds. 'Sir, you will have to wait for your turn,' said the harangued Sergeant as he walked away.

A grim feeling sunk into Kabeer. *'Ayesha is all I have. I cannot lose her'* he thought in panic. His wife Fatima had tragically passed in a hit-and-run case while she was crossing the road near their house 5 years ago. Kabeer was still tirelessly following up with the cops and also the court case to bring the two then underage drunken brats who had so callously taken away his beloved Fatima from him. His frantic calls to some of his juniors in the Air Force who were senior officers now seemed to be of no avail as the Hospital seemed overwhelmed.

Kabeer had retired from Air India for five months now and had just started enjoying his retired life, spending a little more time with Ayesha his only daughter, and catching up on Golf with friends. But the second and devastating wave of COVID had struck again and the last ten days or so had thrown the complete medical support system in the country in general and in Delhi in particular, into a complete shemozzle.

He put SOS messages on the various WhatsApp groups he was in and also on his FB (Facebook) page requesting desperately for an oxygen bed for his daughter. He then frantically dialled a number on his mobile, a last-ditch effort 'Hello Ahlu, can you hear me? Ayesha is in a mess, and I too have fever. BH (Base Hospital) is completely overwhelmed. Need to get Ayesha to a hospital fast, any ideas, bro?' he said amidst a bout of cough. Daljit Ahluwalia a.k.a Ahlu was his batchmate and fellow pilot from the Airforce days and his best friend. He was the quintessential *jugaadu* (street smart) Punjabi from North Delhi and had joined his family business a few years back after retiring from the Air force. If anyone could conjure help in Delhi, it was him.

'Kabeer, honestly things are really bad. Just give me some time and let me work out something. Don't worry we'll make sure nothing happens either to you or Ayesha,' said Ahlu. True to his reputation. Ahlu contacted a Sikh charity which was running a makeshift hospital for COVID care in Punjabi Bagh and was able to manage a single oxygen equipped bed. By the time Kabeer was able to secure the bed and admit Ayesha it was almost morning. His fever too had shot up and he was feeling very weak—though his oxygen levels were still okay. The doctor at the facility admitted Kabeer in the non-oxygen enabled section and he slept fitfully.

It must have been noon when someone shook him awake. It was a male paramedic. 'Sir; is Ayesha your daughter?' he asked. Kabeer nodded. 'Sir, her lungs are infected. You need to move her to an ICU. We will not be able to manage here anymore,' he added shaking his head hopelessly. 'We can manage for a few hours at best, I'm sorry.'

The sinking feeling was back as he called up Ahlu again and also dropped another SOS message in all his WhatsApp Groups. Ahlu promised to do his best. An agonizing 3 hours passed without any luck and Ayesha seemed to be getting worse, though she miraculously was not still that bad.

His mobile rang and the call was from an unknown number. He anyhow picked up the call and mumbled a feeble 'Hello, is this Mr. Kabeer Ahmed?' said the voice from the other end. 'Yes, speaking, who's this please?' said Kabeer. 'Sir, I'm calling from Minerva Hospital Gurgaon. I believe you were looking for an ICU bed,' said the caller. Kabeer couldn't believe his ears. Must be dear old Ahlu's magic at work again he thought.

Things happened in a tizzy after that. The caller took down his location and an ICU ambulance (which too was not available so easily in Delhi at that point of time) fetched up and moved both Ayesha and him to Minerva Hospital, a swanky corporate hospital where they were put up in a separate room equipped with a ventilator and adequate oxygen. He messaged a thank you with folded hands emoji to Ahluwalia for his efforts and largesse and tried calling him. But for some reason the latter did not pick up the phone.

It was a week by the time Ayesha was out of danger and another three days that he tested negative. Ayesha too was well enough to be discharged a week after that. The staff at the hospital had really taken good care of them and surprisingly did not ask for any advance payments etc. as was usually the norm with private hospitals. Ahlu too was for some reason not reachable for all this while.

Finally, the day dawned for them to leave back for home. Kabeer tried Ahluwalia's number yet again. This time he picked up. Ahlu's voice sounded weak and hoarse. 'What happened to you? I have been trying to call you,' said Kabeer. 'Sorry, *paaji* (friend) I too went down with COVID and only just recovering. Had got admitted in Chandigarh as no beds were available in NCR. Still there but getting better. *Aur bata* (and tell me) how are you and Ayesha? Hope all is well.' 'Yes Ahlu, by God's grace and thanks to you—both of us got excellent medical treatment at Minerva Hospital and managed to get out of COVID in one piece.'

'What are you thanking me for? I did nothing, I myself was quite sick,' said Ahlu sounding puzzled. 'Really? Wasn't it you who got us admitted here, and if it wasn't you then who was the good Samaritan who helped us?' said an equally puzzled Kabeer. 'Don't know bro. Anyways what is important is that both of you are okay,' Ahluwalia said before disconnecting.

Kabeer paid off the bills, which he found very reasonable for a hospital of this stature and also during this time when he heard that most private hospitals were making a killing by surging their rates—preying on the panic in the populace. As he and Ayesha turned to leave, a young customer care executive walked up to him and wished him a good morning. 'Sir, hope you had a pleasant stay and are feeling fine now.' 'Yes, of course, thanks to you all and the wonderful doctors here,' said Kabeer with a beaming smile.

'Sir, if you don't mind, our director would like to meet you briefly,' said the young man. Kabeer gave him a puzzled look. 'The Director? Sure,' and followed the executive to what looked like a conference room, wondering as to why the hospital Director wanted to meet him. The executive pushed open the door and he and Ayesha moved into the room. There was only one person in the room—a tall man with a vaguely familiar, Kabeer could not recognise him.

'Kabeer Sir, how are you? I hope you and the young lady are fine,' said the man flashing a smile. Kabeer's mind was now able to rewind and place him; of course, he was Murtaza Hassan—from the Vande Bharat flight!

'I got a forward on my AIIMS Alumni WhatsApp group—basically your SOS message and then thankfully we were able to trace you and Ayesha on time.' said Dr Hassan. 'How can I ever thank you Sir, we are indebted forever to you,' blurted Kabeer, tears welling in his eyes.

'Sir, I should be the one thanking you for what you did, standing up for me on the flight and for the other passengers by risking your life flying us back from the US. It was thanks to you I was able to see my mother one last time and do her last rites. And of course, we as a hospital are indeed honoured to do something for a decorated war hero, this is the least we could do to say thank you—making sure you head safely back home.'

An Ounce of Breath

@Vanshika Gupta

Living for granted in a safe space,
Our minds were set on a role play.
So much chaos in the way,
Shredding the hopes of millions in clay.

Witnessing desolation taking over our lives,
We could have it all if it wasn't for that hike.
How could destiny throw this harsh fate?
Realising it all became too late.

Devoid of hope and fingers crossed,
What once was a beginning
has now reversed its ending.
Pondering over the wrong ways,
A task taken in not so good faith.

Such a little thing called "Life" showed its place,
An irony to be remembered by the generations to stay.
A tiny bit of caution could now save the life game—
Ensuring us to breathe with utmost grace,
Showing the only way out of this catastrophic phase.

But let me tell you, it is not all over yet!
We still have a long way to go, for we still have so much to live
for.
So, hang in there—dear human!
For it isn't easy for sure,
But let us caress our souls,
By vouchsafing a little more of joy to the world!

Chronicles of Lockdown I

@Apoorva Maheshwari

Vidhi looked at her bright computer screen with squinted eyes. The whole room was cast in darkness except for the table where she was sitting. She had been working on a module for her company's upcoming software late into Saturday night. She flipped her phone to look at the time. It was a little past twelve.

Maybe the video call is done. Let's get the phone off flight mode, she wondered as she dragged the top bar to turn off airplane mode and switched on the Wi-Fi.

No sooner had she done that, then there was a shower of text messages. Her phone seemed to come alive with the sounds of the continuous notification alerts. It was as if the simple connection to the Wi-Fi was the elixir that it had been waiting for, for so long. Vidhi's rather annoyed expression was a big contrast to the excited activities of her phone.

She opened the WhatsApp application to find more than a thousand messages in a single group "Cousins v/s Lockdown". Although Vidhi was a member of the group, she was rarely present during any text conversations or video calls. She preferred her secluded life. Her successful career only made it easier for her to maintain the distance. Even her sister left her only voice notes once every two weeks or so.

After deleting all the messages and pictures in the group from that night's video call, without even taking a single peep, she moved on to the other texts. Surely, there was one from her mother, asking her if she had eaten properly, advising her to wear a mask if she went out and reminding her to brush her teeth before she slept. Her mother, a dentist by profession, still left her thirty-year-old daughter reminders to brush and floss her teeth which Vidhi never even acknowledged with a reply.

Finding no work-related texts, she decided to retire for the night. Pleased with herself for making an *optimal use of the time* she put on her pyjamas, brushed, and flossed her teeth, arranged her half a dozen pillows, set an alarm for six in the morning and settled in her bed to sleep.

It was not long before she was woken up by someone gently tapping on her arm. She turned to her left and pulled the blanket higher. But this didn't quite stop the tapping. The frequency of the taps only increased.

'Who is it? What do you want? I want to sleep,' she mumbled in her sleep as she rubbed her eyes. When she opened her eyes, she was startled to see Lucifer, her fashion designer—standing in her room. Perplexed, she pulled her legs close to herself and tried to hide in her blanket.

'Come on darling, you know I am not going to harm you,' Lucifer said in his Australian accent. Lucifer stood there in his flashy pink suit looking down at Vidhi with one hand on his waist.

'What are you doing in my house? How did you get in? And why are you wearing that flashy suit?' Vidhi shot a volley of questions.

'Slow down darling. Let's take one question at a time. I am here to see you. And I am wearing this suit because it's one of my favourites,' explained Lucifer.

'Pink is your favourite colour? You've got to be kidding me,' chuckled Vidhi, 'Are you now going to tell me that you aren't straight?' Vidhi continued laughing.

'Gay is the preferred word darling,' he recoiled with a stern look. 'And yes, it is true. Everyone knows I am happily gay.'

'Oh, what? I never noticed it,' said a puzzled Vidhi.

'Darling, have you ever stopped and smelt the roses along the way? You've missed so many things on the way,' said Lucifer as he patted her back. 'Anyway, time to go.'

'Go where?' asked Vidhi. But it was already too late. Lucifer snapped his finger and now they stood in a small kitchen. It was rather dark because of the lone yellow light that tried its level best to illuminate the room. On the right-hand side there was a sink with a man in grey shorts and a blue t-shirt hunched over.

'Whose house are we in? How did we even get here?' asked Vidhi, shooting more questions.

'Magic darling, magic. As for where we are, you tell me. I have no idea where we are. I was just instructed to bring you here,' explained Lucifer as he scanned the place with a distasteful look.

'We can't move around in other people's houses, Lucifer. What if they see us? We'll be charged with trespassing,' whispered Vidhi as she folded her arms to express her disapproval.

'I know we can't do that. And who said that we are visible? Why don't you take a look at that man and tell me where we are?' Lucifer replied.

Vidhi tippy toed towards the man standing by the sink, cleaning the utensils. It didn't take her long to recognise her who the person was. It was her ex-boyfriend from college, Shashank.

'Alas, I had always known that he was not going to achieve a lot, but I never really imagined that he would be washing dishes like this,' said Vidhi with a sense of pity in her voice.

'He is washing dishes because that's what we all do at night. It's the lockdown period. You should, too, wash those utensils in your sink. Judging by the *Leaning Tower of Pisa* that you have made, I am afraid you might not have utensils even to cook food for tomorrow,' advised Lucifer.

'Baby, leave the utensils, please. I had just gone to pee. You don't have to pamper me so much,' said a sweet voice from the room across.

As Shashank turned around to look at the person with the sweet voice, Vidhi jumped behind the fridge to hide. She even called out to Lucifer indicating another hiding spot.

'We don't have to hide, they can't see us,' Lucifer said as he rolled his eyes.

The woman walked right through Lucifer's wispy form as an astonished Vidhi looked on with her jaw dropped. The woman kissed Shashank on the cheek. Shashank returned the kiss and softly hugged her.

'I have got to, Simran. I can't let the mother of our child work all day and all night. And I need to pamper you twice the usual amount. It's two of you after all,' said Shashank affectionately.

'You are so sweet, Shashank. I am so lucky to have you. You are going to be the world's best father,' said Simran as she moved closer into her husband's arms.

'Aww, they are so cute. Psst—Vidhi who are these people?' asked a love-struck Lucifer.

'That man there is my ex-boyfriend, Shashank. We had dated for three years before I got a job in a big software company and had to move to Bangalore. I asked him if he would come with me, but he said no because he wanted to help his mother take care of his grandmother who wasn't well at the time. I thought he was a complete fool to put his career at stake like that,' explained Vidhi.

'Well, looks like things moved quite well for him, didn't they? He has a wife and is going to have a baby soon. It's such a cute family,' said Lucifer as he intertwined his fingers and rested his head on his hand as he watched the cute couple.

'Let's go Lucifer. I think we have seen enough,' said Vidhi

'Oh, yes darling. We are running out of time,' Lucifer replied as he snapped his fingers. Almost immediately they were transported back to Vidhi's room. Vidhi sat on her bed and switched on the bedside lamp.

'Why did you take me there?' questioned Vidhi. She was evidently sad and hurting.

'Oh, did I not tell you? So silly of me, my apologies. I am playing the ghost of the past,' informed Lucifer.

'Ghost of the past? Like the ghosts in the book "A Christmas Carol"? But it's not even Christmas. And you were pretty much alive when I saw you the last time,' asked Vidhi as she continued to shoot her volley of questions.

'My goodness lady, don't you understand *one question at a time?* I am here to show you what you have missed. There have been so many times when you have been selfish and thought only about yourself. I am here to make you realise that what you think is the ideal life couldn't be further from the truth,' explained Lucifer.

'And who said that one must be helpful, thoughtful, and loving only during Christmas? You should be all of that and more all year round.' scorned Lucifer with his hands on his hips.

'You will be visited by two more people tonight.'

'The ghost of the present and the ghost of the future?' asked Vidhi anxiously.

'Yes, and they'll take you to meet more people. Have a good night, dear. It's time for me to go.' Saying this Lucifer snapped his finger and vanished into thin air.

Vidhi settled down in her bed wondering who the next two visitors might be. Suddenly, she was startled by a cracking sound.

'Don't ask all the questions in one go, darling,' said Lucifer's head which soon disappeared again.

Vidhi tried to control her nerves. She reached out for the glass of water on the side table. With trembling hands, she removed the coaster and brought the glass closer. She took a few tiny sips, looking around the room for any other signs of movement. Unable to make sense of her surroundings, she decided to try to sleep again. She clutched her pillow and drew her legs close to herself, like a wee baby. She pulled her blanket over her head and closed her eyes. All she could do was wait for the next visitor to show up.

To be continued...

Chronicles of Lockdown II

@Apoorva Maheshwari

As her breath became more consistent, Vidhi drifted into sleep. It had been about an hour when she felt a tap on her shoulder. Vidhi, who wasn't in deep sleep, woke up at once. She looked carefully at the person in front of her. She was surprised to find that it was none other than her brother-in-law, Abhay.

'Abhay, what are you doing here,' asked Vidhi.

'I think you know the answer. I am here to take you for your next trip,' replied Abhay. He snapped his finger and soon they stood in front of Abhay and her sister's home.

'Come on in, your sister is just putting the children to sleep,' said Abhay as he tried to open the door. His hand went right through the doorknob.

'Maybe we don't need to open the door,' he said as he walked into the door. Vidhi followed without any protests. She had started getting accustomed to the ghostly ways.

'Ma, you promised us that you'll take us to Bangalore this vacation. We had to meet Vidhi *masi* (aunt). We haven't met her for four years now,' cried the elder of the two children.

'I know Sid, but because of the lockdown, we can't go anywhere, baby. I promise we'll go to see her as soon as the lockdown is over,' said their mother.

'Can we have the photo-photo conversation with Vidhi *masi*? It's been so long. I know she had been busy but during the lockdown surely, she can make some time for us,' said the younger child as her eyes lit up with her brilliant idea.

'It's called a video call Ruhi,' said the older child.

'I'll ask her tomorrow if you promise to sleep right now and do all your online classes tomorrow. Deal?' bargained the mother.

'Pinkie promised Ma,' replied the children in unison. They quickly snuck under the blanket and closed their eyes. Their mother kissed them on the forehead and switched off the light as she left the room.

She then sat at the dining table and held her head in her palms. She clearly looked exhausted. She reached out for the laptop on the table and opened it. She then clicked on the browser icon to open the tabs and browsed through the contents of the page.

'Why is she looking for a job? She had a good job in that start-up na,' asked Vidhi.

'Yes, she did. But because of this extended lockdown, there were many layoffs. She was one of the people who got laid off. Living in a city like Pune doesn't come cheap. We are barely managing right now,' explained Abhay.

'Why didn't you reach out to me? I could have helped you,' asked a sad and hurt Vidhi.

'You haven't really been around these last few years. The only conversations we have had is on Diwali day, that too for about a minute. Vaidehi didn't want to bother you,' replied Abhay.

'I am so sorry Abhay. I had no idea,' lamented Vidhi. 'Siddharth and Ruhi have grown up so much since the last time I saw them.'

'It's been four years you know. Children really grow up pretty fast,' said Abhay with a smile. 'It's time to get you back home,' he said and snapped his finger.

As they reached back to her room, Vidhi was filled with remorse for not keeping in touch with her family. She sat on her bed thinking about what she had just seen.

'I am going to go now. Take care Vidhi. Good night,' said Abhay and vanished.

Vidhi got back into her blanket but couldn't sleep anymore. She took deep breaths to calm herself down but to no avail. She then decided to simply lie in bed as she waited for her next visitor. It wasn't long before the next person appeared. The person was none other than her assistant, Suchita.

'Are you ready to see the next part, Vidhi?' asked Suchita.

Vidhi stepped out of her bed and stood next to Suchita as she nodded in agreement. Suchita snapped her fingers and they soon stood under Vidhi's building. There was an ambulance parked in the lobby.

'Is there a medical emergency, has something happened?' asked Vidhi with genuine concern. Suchita simply pointed at the stretcher that was being brought towards the ambulance. The person on the stretcher looked pale and lifeless. The only person other than the medics accompanying the body was an older Suchita. As she looked closely, the person was none other than herself.

Vidhi was taken aback and almost collapsed. Even in despair she couldn't fall to the ground and floated some inches above it.

'Let's take her to the morgue,' said one of the medics

'Ma'am please inform her family that she has died of a cardiac arrest. They can collect the body from the morgue,' said the other medic.

'I am not sure she has any family. She has never really talked to me about them. I'll check with the office records to see if she has a person of contact listed there,' replied Suchita

'What? I have a family. Do I not have kids? Did I not get married?' asked an astonished Vidhi. She couldn't believe that there was no family member even when she had just died.

'No Vidhi. You didn't get married and have no kids. You were so devoted to your work that you barely had any time for anything or anyone else,' replied Suchita.

'But you are still there! And you don't look so old, too! How old are you when I die?' asked Vidhi desperately.

'You never really ask a woman her age,' retorted Suchita. 'And I think I look around forty.'

'What? This can't be true. I couldn't have died so young?'

'Well, you took no vacations, ate at odd times, kept going, meeting after meeting. You weren't really living a very healthy life. It's actually quite amazing that you lived this long.' Suchita stopped dead in her tracks as she felt Vidhi blankly staring at her.

'This can't be happening. I never planned for this. I didn't want to live or die this way. I wanted to have my own family.' cried Vidhi. Suchita snapped her fingers, and they were back in Vidhi's apartment.

Vidhi jumped on the bed and cried in despair. She wept and wept as Suchita stood there looking at her. Even Suchita was feeling sad for her boss. Soon the tears subsided into sniffles.

'You know Vidhi, that is the future. You aren't dead right now. And by the looks of it, you aren't going to be dead in the next ten-fifteen years at least. You still have a chance to turn it around,' suggested Suchita.

'Hmm,' nodded Vidhi in agreement. 'You know my age?'

'Yes. I am your assistant; remember? And a good one,'

winked Suchita.

Vidhi smiled weakly. It was the first smile of the whole night. She felt reassured that she still had time to turn this whole thing around. She might still have time to have a life.

'Why don't you get some sleep and then you can have a fresh start to the day and to your life,' advised Suchita. 'Good night Vidhi,' said Suchita and vanished. Vidhi took her advice and got into the bed to sleep. For the next few hours, there was no one to wake her up except for her alarm.

As the alarm began to ring, Vidhi jumped out of her bed. She opened the curtains and windows, stretched her arms, and felt the cold breeze. She thanked God for giving her a second chance. She quickly got ready and headed to the kitchen. She then demolished her architecture of utensils and scrubbed and cleaned them. She then looked for her jogging shoes and ran out of the house, only to run back in to fetch her mask.

On her way back, she bought some greens and fresh fruits. At home, she first sanitised all her groceries and made herself a spinach and banana smoothie. She sat on her long unused swing and decided to give her mother a call.

'Hello *Ma*, good morning, how are you? How is Papa doing?' chirped Vidhi.

'Good morning Vidhi. You sound so fresh this morning. What's the secret? And how did you decide to call me today? That too in the morning?' asked her mother in amazement.

'One question at a time, *Ma*. I was missing you so much, so I decided to call you. Where is Papa? I want to talk to him too,' replied Vidhi.

After having a half an hour-long conversation, Vidhi took a bath. She made herself some breakfast and had a glass of milk before she sat down to finish some work. At noon, she decided to make herself a healthy lunch of bottle gourd *sabji* (vegetable) and *chapati* (flat Indian bread). Just as she set her plate on the table, she got a voice note from her sister.

'Hie, Vidhi. How are you? The kids wanted to talk to you for five-ten minutes. Let me know if it's possible for you today. We all miss you a lot.'

Just as the note ended, Vidhi received an email. As she read the contents, she looked pleased with herself. Vidhi forwarded the email to her sister. This time she didn't respond to the voice note with a text message. She opened Duo and made a video call.

'Vidhi, how are you? Did you just send me a job offer letter with your company? How did you know?' asked a puzzled Vaidehi.

'Oh dear, asking a volley of questions runs in the family. It's an early birthday present for you *Di* (sister). Where are Siddharth and Ruhi? I want to talk to them. I miss them so much,' said Vidhi with a big grin on her face. She had just taken baby steps in turning a new leaf.

Sizzling Chef

@Vaishali Chandorkar Chitale

Nobody saw it coming. Like every other New Year—2020 dawned sleepy and hungover. Partying 2019 away, the first day of the year went listlessly moving about the house, planning one's moves (career or otherwise, and looking forward to another rewarding year.

But as they say, 'Man proposes, God disposes!' (Though with a little help from our neighbouring country) and three months into the year, we were locked down in our houses, due to novel coronavirus. Unheard of until then, like the virus that it was, it spread quickly and soon had the eldest to the youngest member of a family in its grip. The often-ignored mammal bat, as if taking revenge for being ignored by mankind for years together, became a hot topic of discussion and internet searches. Words like wet markets, lab-originated, pandemic, global spread, masks, sanitisers, and mutation became household words.

The world as we knew it came to an abrupt halt. Work-From-Home, a not very common phenomenon in our country became the norm. The household help, on whose abled shoulders our family (and country) ran smoothly, ceased coming to work. So effectively, we were all quarantined in our own houses without a relief in sight. Quarantine was another word which one had only heard occasionally; something to do with some communicable diseases, far off from our everyday life, but now it assumed mammoth proportions.

Everybody soon woke up to the fact that a house doesn't run on its own, and all have to contribute to its smooth running. So, how could I be spared? Before I knew it, I was back to doing the only thing I did best. Cooking! Chores of looking after the nutritious intake and making sure the family worked on full stomachs fell into my lap. Never had I imagined that I would enter the kitchen again after handing it over breezily without a backward glance, to my cooks. Incessantly ribbed about my cooking days by my children, I had turned a blind eye to their teasing and refused to entertain their pleas of having *"Maa ke haath ka khana* (meals cooked by mom)". Like an ostrich with its head buried in the sand, I had for many years refused my children's entreating looks to cook for them and had deluded myself into believing that my days on Earth will pass without ever entering its hallowed realms again.

And before I could say 'Never will I ever', I found myself back in the kitchen, making three meals a day for a family of four!

My day usually starts with tea brewed with mint leaves, ginger, and lemongrass—a concoction which I told myself was mandatory to beat all the infections one can catch living in a bustling metropolis. Well, when this handed on a tray to sip with your papers is so welcome, the same becomes so brain numbingly tedious a job when expected to be made every day that I almost started looking lovingly at the polluted air surrounding me and wanted to give up the most- looked-forward moment—my early morning cup of tea and its heavenly sip!

The morning tea ritual would barely be over and the scramble for lunch used to dawn on the horizon with clockwork-like-precision. Soon I realised that God was in cahoots with my children who took perverse pleasure in reminding me that they could not remember my time in the kitchen when they were kids and were now on the verge of forgetting my 'by-now-could-be-extinct' culinary skills. Guess this was their payback time.

I rose magnificently (in my eyes) to the occasion and decided to take up the challenge head on and make my family eat their own words. When I was very active in the kitchen eons ago, social media was still to explode on the scene. I had no record (photos or videos) of whipping up my Michelin starred meals. Now armed with all my tools (Facebook, Instagram, Twitter, YouTube etc.) I had a field day taking pictures and making videos of my lip-smacking delights and uploading them on my accounts. So here I was, as busy as a beaver making all the exotic shahi paneers, biryanis, butter chicken, stuffed bitter gourds, gurer payesh, eggplant risottos, mushroom pastas, chicken Maryland, shepherd's pie etc. and beamed with pride on seeing their incredulous looks. I took to uploading my lockdown creations every day to ostensibly keep a record of my tryst with kitchen again, but mainly to stop the jibes of the family. I also now had virtual proof for the post quarantined days and to look back fondly on my sudden (though forced) creative spurt.

To my immense astonishment I started enjoying my time in the kitchen and glowed in the satisfied burps given soon after. Cooking, they say is like swimming, you never forget. The journey which had started very reluctantly soon became an enjoyable ride and I took to my 'second coming' like fish to water! I started planning meals in advance, rediscovered my skill for disguising the leftovers into a delectable one-pot meals. After all, I was not known as "Leftover Queen" in the family for nothing! My leftover skills are legendary in the family and at all get-togethers, some good-natured ribbing was always on the cards.

I believe in 'zero waste' policy. So obviously, there was a lot of recycling in my kitchen. I had graduated long back from making leftover dal into parathas, that's for novices—I could turn a combination of veggies (including okra and all sorts of gourds, sometimes even bitter gourd) into a vegetable patty for a burger. Leftover rice soon emerged as brand-new spicy pancakes enriched with veggies and garnished temptingly by coriander and cheese, under my guidance. My *theplas* (Indian whole-wheat and pulses flat bread) were a regular guessing game for the family, with them placing bets on the ingredients.

My adventures in the kitchen with some fresh and some leftovers continue and keeps me happily engaged, as this virus seems to be having a field day, spreading with joyful abandon. I understood that God, through this compulsory quarantine, is giving me a chance to redeem myself in the eyes of my ever-suspicious children and this was actually my payback time too!!

Quarantine 2020 has surely been an eye-opener for all of us. It's everybody's guess whether the world as we knew it will come back or a new 'normal' is on the cards. I have understood from this enforced break never take anything for granted. You never know when God is watching from above.

Never say never—I learnt it the hard way!!

****

PS: The maids are back in the kitchen, this now being circa 2022, but I am still making my version of delectable meals, much to the astonishment of my family.

DNA in a Soup I

@Deepti Sharma

The RNA stirred lazily in his sleep. He was dreaming pleasantly in the dead of the cellular night, as he floated in the cytoplasm, safe within the confines of the cell membrane. He dreamed of the billions of years old primordial soup—delightfully free of the new-fangled oxygen and ozone. Methane, hydrogen, ammonia—how the RNA loved them. There was lightening, electric sparks, acid pools, meteors colliding with the earth, and various organic chemicals paying homage to him. The carbohydrates were particularly obsequious, especially the glucose and the fructose, for they were in full cognisance of the crucial roles they'd be playing later in gazillions of cells. At the RNA's behest, naturally. The lipids, historically humble creatures who knew they were important but not critical, bent low to show especially deep gratitude for being permitted to the royal presence. The amino acids bowed assiduously, though not all the 500 odd ones, of course. Most of the D-amino acids were still nursing a grudge against the RNA for they had not been the chosen ones. Ah well, one can't please everyone. The top 20 amino acids that would be selected (millions of years later in the future) to be part of that supreme organism—the *Homo sapiens*—loved the RNA unconditionally. Tryptophan, alanine, arginine, cysteine—everyone adored RNA. But the RNA returned the affection of a very few. Very few were *worth* the RNA's regard. For instance, the RNA detested the proteins very much, heartless wenches that they were, who couldn't decide whose side they were on.

And then the RNA's dream took an even more pleasant turn. His strongest and truest and staunchest acolytes, the RNA-viruses had emerged. Rhinovirus, the many flu viruses, HIV, Corona, Ebola, Rabies, Polio, the Hepatitis Viruses—hundreds of them milling about. Hundreds of these noble creatures who had enclosed the RNA within the warmth of their protein folds, who had lived with the RNA inside them for billions of years, who literally worshipped the RNA! One chant united all the RNA-viruses in their deep devotion for this ancient hereditary strand.

O RNA! Our Lord!

May your Adenine-Uracil bond live long

May your Guanine-Cytosine bond prolong

May you replicate ever so wisely

Not like foolish DNA, but so precisely

May you again rule the earth

Create species that have the worth

At peace and eternally simple

In the cellular skies you twinkle

The RNA smiled in his sleep as notes of this hymn echoed in his mind.

The Endoplasmic Reticulum bumped rudely into the floating RNA, pulling him out of deep slumber.

'Mr Ribonucleic Acid?' The ER tended to be formal in his speech.

'Eh, what?' For the RNA was still groggy. Most manifestations of the RNA—the RNA had several avatars - did not float freely in the cytoplasm. Instead, these r-RNA or ribosomal RNA remained seated on the ribosomes, which, in turn, stuck to the ER. For this reason, RNA was a little fond of the ER. Woken up by any other cell organelle, RNA would have let his wrath loose on the hapless victim.

'Mr Deoxyribonucleic Acid has been sending urgent signals for you. Since past several cell-seconds.'

RNA, wide awake now, knew that even one cell-second was precious and critical for the survival of the cell. One cell-second ticked away much quicker than the seconds of the world outside. The urgency tautened RNA's entire length even as he glided over the ER and passed directly into the nuclear pore, seeking admission into the DNA's palace, the nucleus. These nuclear pores were very selective—not every chemical was permitted entry—for the safety of the cell's young emperor, the DNA, was at stake here. But for the RNA, there were no access restrictions. At least not yet.

'There you are, you doddering old fool,' DNA's arrogant voice boomed, echoing ominously from all corners of the nucleus. You see, the nucleus was choked full of chromosome—a hybrid formed by DNA's associations with many proteins, the proteins being the silent partners. There was simply too much of DNA in the nucleus, and barely room for any other chemical to stand.

'It's taken you eons to come down here. Is age catching up with you?'

Taken aback by the emperor's sneering tone, the RNA remained quiet.

'Where were you? Dreaming of the primordial soup if I am not wrong. And of the viruses, too. I know you are a traitor, RNA. You love the viruses that annihilate our cells.'

The accuracy of the guess further stunned the RNA, preventing speech.

'Are we deaf now? Incapable of communication?'

The RNA found his voice, finally. 'Not at all, Emperor DNA. Viruses tend to love me more than I love them. After all, I run the whole show inside them. But I can never allow a virus to harm our cells. Now, let me know what the royal command is, and I'd deliver, as always.'

The DNA gave an unpleasant laugh.

'Hah, yes. Like a tribal demigod, aren't you, for those foolish little viruses? Anyway, I need to start replicating soon, and unfortunately, there is no way for me to do so without your involvement. I need you to fetch your primers and get into action immediately.'

'What? Replicate again? We had replicated not long before.'

'So now you are going to dictate my replication cycle, you fossil?' The RNA stood his ground politely but firmly. 'Emperor DNA; do not forget that I am far older than you. I have seen billions of species come and go. Evolution has its own rules. Over-replication and over-population can undo a species. Look at the dinosaurs. Do you want the *Homo sapiens* to perish?'

The DNA was enraged beyond words. Before the RNA could finish his last few words, the emperor had unleashed a shower of uridine bombs on his vulnerable minister. The RNA strands broke down within no time. The DNA's laughter echoed frighteningly in the nuclear chamber. It took the RNA several cell-seconds to reassemble his structure.

'So, did you get your senses back? Shall we start replicating now?'

The RNA nodded mutely. Replication was a painful process.

The RNA had to summon many of his primer incarnations at

the same time and help the polymerase protein perform her magic of copying two DNA strands into four. It took hours of toil on the part of the others, while throughout this process the DNA had to do nothing other than unwinding luxuriously, consuming the resources, fattening up, and dividing into the daughter strands.

And it is not as if the RNA's troubles would end with the replication process. The newly formed daughter cells would need essential proteins. Protein formation also required RNA to work like a stevedore. All in all, it would be an exhausting cell-day for RNA, the ex-emperor.

****

The RNA was in high dudgeon. Really, was there no limit to which the DNA would go? No respect for the eons and eons of age-gap between them. No regard for the billions of replication cycles that separated them. Indeed, millennia had passed when RNA had ruled as the only—only genetic material. Ah, those were the days. Naturally, he deserved more respect, more honour. Besides, wasn't the RNA still indispensable for the cell?

'Only the fool will denigrate my role in the evolution of life,' RNA told ER and the ribosomes. 'Why, just look at my diversity of form—m-RNA, t-RNA r-RNA, so many incarnations to choose from.'

The ribosomes nodded in agreement while the ER, with his gigantic tubular structure, could only vibrate slightly.

'Multi-tasking begins with me folks, with me. I invented the term. I *evolved* the very concept. See you, I replicate as the only hereditary material in ancient cells. I ensure proper protein formation in all the modern DNA-bearing cells. I even catalyse reactions like proteins.'

'But then Mr RNA, you shouldn't have given over the control to Mr DNA. Why did you?' ER asked curiously.

The RNA looked a tad uncomfortable. 'Not my fault. Look at this evolution. Darned headstrong old wench. Bent on making everything complex. No respect for simplicity. Tell me, what was wrong with a world full of viruses? Can the *Homo sapiens* say they are better than a virus? No, they are just more complex than one. I couldn't handle complex creatures all by myself. I had no option but to bow down to the evil but more efficient DNA.'

'But even in these complex species, you Mr RNA, have an undeniably critical role to play,' the ER went on, in awe of the ex-emperor.

'Hah, yes. Look at how I control DNA in humans—98% of their DNA is "junk", coding for *me*—I let only 2% of the human genome code for proteins. And yet look at my simplicity. Unpretentious, unadorned, unembellished, austere even, that's me. *I* am not vulgar like this deoxyribonucleic acid, flaunting its stability, replicating unhindered, eating up all the resources. Why, these DNA cells, especially the humans, have over-populated the planet. So many of my virus friends are lost, thanks to these evil superior strands.'

The mitochondria floated by, a gigantic pulsating presence, the powerhouse of the cell where respiration went on. Evolutionary history had proof of the DNA-bearing cell's atrocities on the mitochondria. Indeed, the mitochondria was an independent entity before being subjugated, overpowered, and enslaved by the DNA, forced to perform the respiratory duties for providing the emperor's replication energy. The mitochondria's anger had piled up over the centuries.

'I hear you, Mr RNA. Loud and clear. I have remained angry at the DNA for so many years now. But I am powerless to do anything.'

The RNA nodded moodily.

'Look at my karmic cousins, the plastids, in the plant cells,' said mitochondria. 'Forced to perform photosynthesis in there, just as I am getting grilled in the Kreb's cycle. Poor plastids seem to have forgotten their proud, independent past. With me, I have the curse of memory. I can't even forget.'

A lysosome, the cellular suicide bag, flitted by and the mitochondria grew more melancholy still upon seeing him. 'Sometimes I feel I ought to instigate these lysosomes to burst near me and finish me off with their bag full of digestive enzymes. I am tired of this slave's life.'

The ER, the ribosomes and the RNA started speaking at once, attempting to cheer up the mitochondria and remind him of its crucial role in cellular survival. Even the Golgi apparatus, a sworn taciturn but with very sharp ears, came over to offer his advice on shedding suicidal thoughts.

Once the mitochondria had floated away, slightly more cheerful than before, the Golgi apparatus settled quietly near the RNA.

'Mr RNA, don't you feel it is high time the DNA was taught a lesson?'

'What do you mean, Golgi?'

'I mean that it is time to unleash your centuries old forces.'

'My dear Golgi, I am just a *doddering old fool* as the emperor is so fond of calling me. I have no powers now. Just responsibilities and duties. They say power without responsibility corrupts. But then I'd like to ask, what is the fate of those with responsibilities without power?'

'Mr RNA, you forget your powerful devotees. Your viruses. For them, it is child's play to mutate and jump from cell to cell. Why, they could twist the DNA strands the other way round if you wanted them to. Look at the human DNA—it has not retained its evolutionary relation with any of its sister species.

Not even with the closest apes. In fact, the fools are busy destroying their own brethren. Not so with your army of RNA viruses. They will all stand up as one, at but one call from you.'

'But I am no traitor, Golgi. I cannot wage a war against my own cell and destroy it.'

'Ah, well. You are old and wise. I am but a novice, a mere packer of proteins into vesicles. Far be it from me to advise you. But why should the human cell be destroyed? Most of your acolytes are smart to punish just enough and not too much.'

The Golgi apparatus bid goodbye, leaving behind an RNA that was very pensive.

To be continued...

DNA in a Soup II

@Deepti Sharma

The RNA kept chewing on the Golgi's words even as it helped the new daughter cells get their regular supply of necessary proteins. Its m-RNA and t-RNA avatars were very active and allowed it to think unhindered. And the more he thought, the more sensible Golgi's words sounded. Yes, why shouldn't the RNA strands of the world unite and rebel against the DNA? Why shouldn't DNA supremacy be challenged? Why shouldn't the evolutionary race to complexity be checked a little by humble simplicity? Why shouldn't the RNA win again?

But it would need a plan. A meticulous, well-devised plan. The human DNA was crafty and knew well how to protect itself. There had to a novel virus, one that the human DNA had never encountered before. And the virus had to be an accomplished shapeshifter, mutate like lightening, but not foolishly. Just enough to evade the attack of vaccines, but not so much that they destroyed themselves.

The RNA began to meditate, sending out signals of telepathy to all the RNA viruses of the world, commanding them all to connect with him and with each other.

RNA viruses of the world unite!
Your parent strand calls upon you
Stand as one against the DNA oppressors
Come, the world needs you
Come, it is now time to fight!

The influenza virus types and subtypes were the first to respond. Able mutators, they had beguiled and confused the human DNA for years. Why, the humans had had to take vaccination shots every year just to evade the multi-faceted flu virus! H1N1 outbreak was pretty recent in human memory.

'Emperor RNA, we are at your beck and call. Tell us, which DNA do we tear apart and take up as our own?' The robust, spherical flu monsters intoned with gusto.

'My friends, the flu viruses, it is so good to see you!'

The hepatitis viruses A, B, C, D and E did not like each other. They felt they were too different from one another to be clubbed together unceremoniously. And hence, they had joined the meeting as separate entities, unlike the influenza virus that always kept the herd of its types and subtypes together under one banner. Problem was, they always wanted to talk together, A to E, and it was impossible to make out five different sentences spoken at once. After trying to make sense of their words for several cell-seconds, the RNA had to put them all on mute.

The bullet-shaped rabies virus, as angry as it made its victims, had logged into the tele-talk from the driest desert of the world. 'I want to rid the world of mammalian DNA. Oh, how I hate their nerves!'

'My dear rabies, I hope you're doing good! Outmanoeuvred the vaccine yet?'

The mighty HIV, which had aimed to threaten the human speed of reproduction, sounded weary. 'I am there, Emperor, with all my heart. But I have tried my might and failed.'

'My friend, you scared the humans good and proper. They are still hunting for a credible vaccine against you.'

The rare and deadly Ebola virus was very straightforward. 'Emperor, I infect to kill. I don't know how you'd like to employ me, but I really can't control my killer instincts.'

'Ebola, my friend, I understand. We RNA viruses are out to survive at the cost of others, though not too high a cost. But your rarity balances your deadliness.'

The humble rhinovirus, Ebola's exact opposite in being too common and too mild, knew well that it had no use in this war against the DNA. But it had connected nevertheless, in the hope of paying obeisance to the emperor.

The tiny polio virus whimpered feebly, 'Ah, Emperor and my fellow RNA friends! How good to see you even as my vision fades! These humans—their vaccines against me have brought me on my deathbed. Very soon I will have to big goodbye to all of you. But even with my dying breath, I shall pray for your success.'

'My precious ally—how can we forget you? Weren't you the one that crippled humanity and brought it down to its knees not too long ago? So what if the vaccines slowly won against you? You did your job well.'

The RNA cogitated upon the available options. It would be best to get viruses that could enter via the respiratory pathway. Food or waterborne ones and those that were transmitted via body fluids or by animal or insect bites could be fended off by the human DNA with relative ease. Also, there was no point employing viruses that were not mutating quick enough to evade the vaccines. At the same time, the viruses needed to cause stress, but not death. So, a very deadly virus was not an option here either.

Flu viruses were a good option, but the human race was well-prepared against them. Getting annual shots against the invasion was a hassle but not a worry. He wanted the DNA to be acutely stressed.

The coronavirus had been having connectivity issues, for the geography where it was currently active had heavily guarded information transmissions of any kind. Finally, it got its voice across.

'Emperor RNA, trust me, I am your best option. I have just managed to jump across one mammalian cell to another, and after my last mutation, I think my protein capsule has become smart enough to infect human DNA. I can spread very fast from cell to cell, faster than the flu or rhinovirus, and my infection is definitely deadlier.'

The RNA nodded, 'Yes corona, you do look like a promising option. Go! Wreak havoc on the DNA world!'

****

And so, a reign of viral terror was let loose. Infections spread from country to country in no time. Within weeks, nearly all the nations of the world came to a screeching halt, the human DNA controlling its earlier unchecked urge to consume resources. Millions of infected individuals created panic across the globe.

Corona was a naughty virus though, and initially its deadliness was more than what the RNA had bargained for. However, corona was also an obedient virus and very loyal to the RNA. One admonishing lecture from the emperor, and the corona began to mutate towards decreased virulence.

But luckily by that time, its terror had spread enough to all the corners of the earth. Humans had begun to stay indoors, scared of over-consumption. RNA's job was done and done well.

****

The Golgi apparatus and the RNA were sharing a knowing smile when the ER vibrated and informed the ex-emperor about the summons from the nuclear palace.

'Emperor DNA wants you, Mr RNA.'

'I will go at once, ER. Just help me slide into the nuclear pore closest to you.'

Once inside the royal presence, the RNA was pleasantly surprised to find the DNA sound soft and polite.

'Ah, RNA, there you are.'

'How are you now, emperor? I trust that the corona strands are now out of your system, and you are back to normal?'

'Yes, oh, yes. But when I remember those stressful days, RNA, my soul shrinks in fear. I've learnt my lesson, RNA, I'd say I've learnt my lesson full and well.'

'What lesson, emperor?'

'What you have been saying since ages. Takes just a single RNA strand from a vicious source to turn me into a cripple, doesn't it? Look at me—leaving aside my own replication, I'd been replicating those very viral strands that were synthesizing proteins to harm me. In short, the virus had plagiarised my replication system. So, am I better than a virus? No way, I am just more complex than one. Does complexity win over simplicity? Nah, it's the other way round in so many ways. You know my new quest, RNA?'

'What, emperor?'

'Simplicity within complexity—I cannot undo my complexity, but I am going to adopt simplicity and slow down as much as I can.'

'Sounds good, emperor.'

'You may go now, RNA, and take a dip in the primordial soup of your dreamy past.'

****

The zephyrs were pleased
The gaping sky hole sealed,
Bowels of the waters
Finally cleansed.

Spring in the turtle flaps
The cuckoo piercingly squawks,
Cocking its head, "Caged?"
It seemingly asks.

It was one against ten million
But the others were mere minions,
Dried, depleted, resources drained
Was earth just man's dominion?

Cure for the earth, curse for the ruler
Came a vicious invisible intruder,
Pulling down the despot to his knees
A fate befitting the abuser.

Shall we win? What if we do?
Toast to our older greedier hue?
Or dare we hope of lessons learnt,
A golden earth that did pull through.

Homeless in Pandemic

@Monika Patel

Last night as I was unwinding and looking at next day's schedule on my smart phone, up popped a message to take a look at the pictures of 'This day, that year'. I tapped on my phone and was flooded with memories from the year 2020.

The year 2020 began on a very positive note for our family, we celebrated my father's seventy-fifth birthday on January 1, with a grand party. Little did we know that for the next two years rest of us are going to be home bound for our birthday celebrations. The beginning of the year also coincided with me taking a sabbatical and registering for master's program in special education. All in all, things were looking good. One important task that needed attention was the renovation of our house in Mumbai where we live. It was on my priority list to get the work done before my full-time college began in June. The year that we had started on a very positive and hopeful note soon turned into a living nightmare. Each one of us has experienced lockdown in our own unique way. Here is my peculiar lockdown story.

I must begin before the pandemic was declared and the lockdown was announced.

The place where we had been living for the last ten years

desperately needed a makeover. Somehow the *mahurat* (auspicious time) to get the work started never seemed to come. There were multiple reasons for it—one among them being whether to live in and get the work done or move out to a rented place. The discussion about the same never seemed to end. We decided to live in and get the work done one room at a time.

Finally in the month of February 2020 the work started. It was going to be an uphill task of getting the work done while living in the same house as the repairs were major and needed bringing down the plaster and the false-ceiling and doing the bathrooms from scratch. Fortnight into the work the architect informed us that as plumbing in both the bathrooms will have to be done simultaneously, we will have to move out for at least three weeks. So, it was decided that I and my husband would move to a hotel nearby. We were good with that. The plan was that while the kitchen and the rest of the work gets done, we will eat out and accommodate in the available space.

So far so good

We shifted to a hotel not far from our house, because of the proximity we were able to visit the site daily. Talks of virus hit China had started to make rounds but I simply did not foresee the gigantic situation that awaited us all. Quite unaware, we continued with our expedition of renovation, breaking down the kitchen completely, to even uprooting the tiles to lay down new pipelines. Holi holidays happened. Unfortunately, the repairs never really gained the same momentum after the break, as the workers who had left for Holi did not come back because of the talks of the lockdown.

While we were still staying at the hotel, I had received a call from a good friend, mother of my twins' friend. She suggested we shift to her empty one room flat, if need be. I had never thought

I would have to get in touch with her to live in her house. But then, after Holi when the work didn't resume, we had no choice but to take up the offer. We shifted to Poonam's flat with our clothes, some crockery and hope that we will be out of here in maximum months' time.

As we reached mid-March, words like pandemic, lockdown, quarantine, self-isolation, epidemiologist, virus, social distancing were being used widely and frequently.

My children were asked to head home from their respective universities by mid-March, my son came back home, but my daughter went to stay with my parents for the next three months, as we had no 'home'.

We shifted to Poonam's house exactly a week before the lockdown was announced in March 2020. We can never thank Poonam enough for letting us stay in their house. We were majorly dependent on delivery services for our food. Days passed in a blur initially, not able to understand what lay ahead. At the onset it was said the lockdown will be for a fortnight; I waited patiently for the fortnight to end and the work in my broken-down house to resume. My patience was tested for more than a year before the work began again.

We gradually started to settle down. We had no groceries or utensils to cook and mercifully the food services continued undisrupted, so we survived. We lived on hope that things will be back to normal in a fortnight. We had collected a lot of cooked food when the announcement was made. Couple of days earlier I had got loads of dry snacks. So, began our lockdown with a refrigerator full of cooked food. Watching news on TV became a religious practise. We survived on daily home delivery of hotel cooked food till the end of March. Then I put my foot down about eating from restaurants.

One afternoon I and my husband walked to our broken down house and ventured into the room where we had piled up all our belongings. Thankfully, I had labelled them. I got hold of some essential utensils and returned with a heavy heart—our home looked deserted and sad. Thankfully, there was a piped gas connection and a refrigerator in Poonam's house. I started cooking at home. That kept me busy cause once I started cooking there were utensils to clean and meals to plan and the biggest expedition of all—to get the supplies. Another chore that needed to be carried out was getting the clothes washed. Before the lockdown I used to go once a week to my sister-in-law's place and get the clothes washed, we had to find a solution—my son and husband went to our under-construction flat, assembled the washing machine and the dryer, and it became my son's job to get the clothes washed from then on. He would carry the soiled clothes, wash, and dry them and bring them back. He did it for the entirety of our stay.

Some incidents will remain etched in my memory forever.

Day or two after the first lockdown was announced, I and my husband ventured out on the streets, mission being to hoard some food. The roads were mostly deserted—some random couples like us and very few vehicles on one of the busiest roads. We must have walked around five hundred steps when we could hear the police car approaching. We were bang opposite a temple when the police car stopped right next to us and the officer on duty yelled into his microphone to make us stop and to inquire where we were headed. Both of us were scared and embarrassed to be screamed at. When we told him that we were out to get groceries and essentials we got another earful from him and were informed that only one person from a family can go out at a time. He asked us to go home immediately and told us not to find excuses for breaking the lockdown rules. I was quite perplexed. We never ventured out together again in the first lockdown, after that incident. I used to go and get stuff by myself, but carrying heavy bags had its cons. A solution was devised. I walked back home empty handed, and my son would go and pick up the bags on his bike. Thank God for our children.

Another time I ventured out in the first week of the lockdown was for medicines. It was about half past five in the evening and the road opposite to the Parleshwar Temple was deserted, with not a soul in sight. The silence was eerie. I was shaken by the sight of this always overcrowded road being deserted. I rushed back without bothering to get the stuff I needed.

The sights of migrant workers travelling on foot and crowding at the train stations to get back home will remain etched in our memories. The whole episode was heart wrenching and watching news day in and day out, I learnt to count my blessings. I thanked God hundred times a day for a roof over my head, however inconvenient it was.

Time flew by. Day after day, week after week and month after month. The pandemic made us aware of our capabilities, our endurance and patience. I had never thought that I could do all the household work by myself. It has made me ever so grateful for all the house help I have had. Our house help suffered too, family members tested positive, the uncertainty and worry were at the doorstep and the intense sense of uncertainty and helplessness became a constant.

I had enrolled for my master's degree, in the BC (Before Corona) era, now in the AC (After Corona) era it all seems like a far stretched dream.

But I did not lose hope, I believed I will be reunited with my daughter and my parents soon. I was also looking forward to seeing some of my school friends whom I got in touch with during those few months. One massive blessing was a stray kitten who made our house, his home.

I realised how little we needed in terms of materialistic things.

I had learnt to cook with a couple of utensils. I pondered over my intense need for a bigger kitchen with huge storage space, one of the reasons for which we had started the renovation of our house in the first place. To this day, I keep contemplating if any of those needs, wants and wishes mean anything at all.

I brood over a lot of other things. Covid has given me a lot of time to ruminate.

I realised that you could plan all you want, but sometimes you have to leave everything to fate and wait for the time to be right again.

PS: We could start the work for our house only in 2021. We were back in our house with Chibi, our adopted kitten. He has brought tremendous joy to our lives; he is our blessing in disguise from that profoundly terrible experience.

As they say tough times never last, tough people do. And no doubt, after what we went through, we have become strong enough to take on any challenge that circumstances throws at us.

Shoaib—A Tale of Fear

@Zeyd Ladha

'Guys, so it's confirmed. 18th March we catch up for dinner,' said Varun on a conference call with his friends. Shoaib, Rahul, Varun, Joseph, and Rohan—all in their mid-forties, had been the best of friends. They stayed in the same building in Mumbai and would regularly go out for a drink or dinner. This was their plan on the 18th of March 2020. As always, they had a great time and decided to go out again the following week. Little did they know, life was about to change forever. Covid-19 was spreading rapidly throughout the world, but it's human nature to ignore an issue till it actually knocks on your door.

With the number of cases in the financial capital of India steadily on the rise, the government of Maharashtra announced a complete lockdown in the state for 14 days. It brought mixed reactions from people. Some were very concerned while others looked forward to a short 14-day staycation.

'Hi Varun,' said Shoaib on call.

'Hey! What's up?'

'Listen, let's go and get groceries for the next few days. It's a complete lockdown and I'm not sure if we will get anything later,' said Shoaib, sounding terribly worried.

'Listen Shoaib, firstly, calm down! You're not going to run out of food, essential services will continue to function as always. Secondly, we are here brother. You need anything you know whom to call! Now calm down, you will make your family tense too.'

'Thank you, brother, but let's just go get whatever we can.'

'Okay,' replied Varun, 'let's go.'

Varun called up the others in their group, specifically asking them to be positive and happy and try to calm Shoaib.

So, the guys met in the building compound. For some time, they stayed there and spoke about current affairs. They shared their point of views on the situation, but Shoaib did not speak a word. He just kept wiping the sweat off his brow and nervously played with his mobile phone.

'What's wrong Shoaib?' Asked Joseph.

'Yeah, you don't look so good,' added Rohan.

'I'm okay,' Shoaib replied in a soft voice.

'Listen Shoaib, we all our worried too. Your stress is legitimate, but you need to try and relax. Your family will look up to you, if you break down, what will they do?' said Varun.

'But guys, it is a matter of concern, isn't it? Like we cannot step out of the house for 14 days,' said Rahul.

'Listen guys,' said Joseph, 'you know I have a bungalow in Khandala. My family and I are leaving for Khandala tonight. If any of you wish to join us, you guys are most welcome.'

'Wow, Lucky you. Have a great vacation,' said Varun.

Shoaib had been a silent spectator during the entire conversation.

'Let's go get the groceries,' said Shoaib, finally saying something, the only thing he had said since the lockdown was announced.

'Yes, let's go,' said Varun and they started walking to the store.

The scene at the store was so horrific, all of them felt uneasy and Shoaib got even more tensed. People had thronged the store. Hundreds of men and women falling over each other trying to get hold of basic necessities.

'Damn!' exclaimed Shoaib perplexed. 'Let's go to the other store on the back road. It's at a secluded location and is generally not crowded,' he added.

So, the five of them walked to the other store. To their horror, the scene was no different here. In fact, it was worse at this store. A heated argument broke out between a couple of customers which led to a fight.

'What do we do?' Asked Varun.

'I'm going in to get what I want,' said Shoaib.

The others just looked at each other for a moment and the Varun spoke. 'Brother you need to calm down. Let's just go home. I have a big stock of groceries at home, you can take from me.'

'Thank you but let me try if I can get something.'

'I'll come with you,' said Rahul.

The duo dived and after must hustle and bustle returned looking like a couple of wrestlers exiting the ring after a long gruesome fight.

'We hardly got anything. Most of the things are out of stock already! This is crazy. The government should have given us a couple of days to prepare,' complained Shoaib.

They started walking back towards their building.

As they reached the gate, Varun whispered in Rahul's ear, 'Shoaib is freaked out. He hasn't spoken a word since we left from the store.'

'Yeah. I hope he is able to manage his feelings better.'

'Hope so!' replied Varun.

They tried to involve Shoaib in their conversations, but he hardly spoke. They retired to their respective homes, for how long no one knew. Joseph left for Khandala within an hour. Shoaib and his wife, Zainab, waived Joseph's family off from their balcony. Then started the dreaded time when no one could step out of the house. That was a time of mixed emotions and feelings. There were those who made the most of it by spending time with their kids. Others took to fitness challenges, uploading their fitness routine videos on social media websites. Some learnt baking, others learnt how to cook a new dish. While many were busy trying to use the time productively, there were some, like Shoaib, who were glued to their television sets watching news channels. Media did little to comfort people. Shoaib's fear went from bad to worse. Their building had organised a vegetable vendor to come to their premises once every four days. Men and women would come down to buy their vegetables and fruits. It was also a much-needed respite from solitude. For a few minutes people met, spoke a little, laughed a little and for those few moments, forgot they were in the midst of a pandemic.

One day when the vegetable vendor came, Rahul and Shoaib did not come down.

'Let's call them,' said Varun.

First, he called Rahul.

'Hey Rahul! Don't you want vegetables?' asked Varun.

'Brother, I need a favour,' he replied.

'Tell me.'

'I am down with cough and fever, and I think it might be Covid-19,' said Rahul. 'Can you drop the vegetables outside my door, ring the doorbell and walk away?'

'Sure brother. Shouldn't you get tested though?'

'I visited the lab this morning. Isolating till I get the results tomorrow. If it's positive, I'll get myself admitted.'

'Very responsible!' said Varun.

Then he called Shoaib a couple of times, but Shoaib did not answer and then Varun got busy with shopping for himself and for Rahul. The next day, Rahul called Varun in the morning.

'Hey Rahul, hope you're fine?' asked Varun.

'I have tested positive!' replied Rahul. Varun sat up straight in bed. After a minute of silence he said, 'What's the next step now?'

'I got a call from the local municipal corporation. I have taken a bed at the super speciality private hospital. The ambulance should be here any minute,' said Rahul.

'Listen Rahul,' said Varun, 'if there's anything you need or if there's anything *Bhabhi ji* (sister-in-law) and the kids want please do not hesitate to call me. We are a family. You got that?'

'Yes! Thank you so much, brother, and you know what?'

'What?' asked Varun.

'*I will be back!*' said Rahul in typical Arnold Schwarzenegger swagger.

'Hahaha!' laughed Varun, 'I'm sure you will brother! God bless you.'

At noon, the ambulance arrived and a couple of PPE clad men escorted Rahul to the ambulance. There was a hush in the society. There was fear in the hearts of people. Some thought this was a one-way trip to the hospital. Those like Shoaib, who saw too much of the news feared the consequences of being hospitalised. Some thought it was a conspiracy to control human population. Shoaib and Zainab were watching this from their balcony. Shoaib did not look too well, and Varun noticed this.

A couple of days later the vegetable vendor was back and again there was no sign of Shoaib. Again, Varun called and yet again he did not answer. Now Varun was concerned.

'Should we go to his place and check on him?' Varun asked Rohan.

'I don't think that's a good idea in today's scenario. Let's wait a couple of days, if we don't hear from him, we'll go and check on him,' said Rohan.

'Fair enough,' replied Varun.

Late that night, Varun's phone rang. He searched for the light switch, still in sleep. He then got up and checked his phone.

'Zainab!?' He said and woke his wife up.

'Hello,' he answered the call.

'Hello Varun,' she said and couldn't speak further. She started crying on call.

'Zainab, why are you crying? What's the matter?' He asked, obviously very worried.

But she continued to sob.

'Hold on, we are coming,' said Varun. His wife quickly got ready, and they called Rohan as well. They rushed to Shoaib's house. They knocked and took a few steps back. Zainab opened the door, still crying.

'What is the matter, Zainab?' Asked Varun.

'Yes, please tell us what happened,' added his wife.

'Look,' said Zainab, fully openly the door. They were shocked to see a pale looking Shoaib panting for breath, lying helplessly on the couch.

'Oh my god! What happened?' Asked Varun.

'He's been running a temperature for past 6 days and he's coughing as well, but he refuses to see the doctor or get himself tested,' replied Zainab. 'He's been unwell even before Rahul. Rahul, I believe, is in hospital and recovering. Shoaib on the other hand thinks those who go to hospital never return. Look, now look at his condition,' she added and broke down.

Times were such, they could only see her cry. They could neither give her a shoulder to cry on nor give her a hug to make her feel better. Covid had taken people away from each other like no one ever could.

'We have to do something!' said Varun.

'Should we call an ambulance?' asked Rohan.

They tried but in vain. After fifteen minutes, they noticed Shoaib's health deteriorating quickly. Varun ran to the medical store and got a couple of PPE kits. Rohan and he put on the kits and went into Shoaib's house. They picked Shoaib up and took him to Varun's car. They put him in the back seat and rushed to the super-speciality hospital. They admitted him in covid emergency and waited outside. Zainab and Varun's wife arrived a few minutes later. The doctors asked them to go home and come back the next morning. Once home they discarded the PPE kits outside the house and went straight to the washroom to take a wash with hot water with antiseptic liquid. Varun and Rohan's families were worried for them. They had handled what seemed to be a certain case of Covid-19. But what choice did they have? They could not see their dear friend struggle for life right in front of their eyes.

The next morning, they reached the hospital. The doctor came out to meet them.

'You are?' asked the doctor.

'I am Varun, Shoaib's friend. This is Zainab, his wife and that's Rohan, a friend, too.'

'So, I will not beat around the bush,' said the doctor. 'He is in critical condition.'

Zainab broke down. Rohan tried to console her.

'Infection has spread to his lungs. We keep telling people early testing saves lives! But some don't listen. We have put him on the best medication available and some steroids, let's hope he responds,' said the doctor.

Varun took the doctor aside and asked, 'What do we expect, Doctor?'

'I really can't say at the moment. Let's see how he responds to medication. We will keep you updated,' replied the doctor.

'And what about Rahul who is also admitted here?' asked Varun.

'Rahul Sharma, right?' asked the doctor flipping the pages of his file.

'That's right,' replied Varun.

'He's doing good. He checked early and came soon. I'll take your leave now.'

Varun went to the water cooler and got Zainab a glass of water. Zainab was still crying. They made her sit on a bench.

'Zainab, I know it's difficult, but you have to be strong. We all are praying, nothing will happen. Have faith in Allah,' consoled Varun.

'Excuse me,' said a nurse. 'As per covid guidelines, only one person can wait outside the hospital. Others, please go home.'

'Sure sister,' replied Varun.

'Zainab, you go home with Rohan. Your kids are alone at home. I will stay back,' said Varun.

'How can I go home Varun?' said Zainab, 'While Shoaib is in this condition.'

'There isn't much you can do here. Rather than waiting here

in this heat, go home and be with your kids. They need you. Rohan, please both of you go home.'

Rohan and Zainab left for home. A couple of hours later, while Varun was having lunch in the cafeteria, he received a call from the doctor asking him to come to the ward immediately as Shoaib was critical. Varun took the stairs not wanting to waste time waiting for the elevator.

'What happened doctor?' asked Varun, panting for breath.

'His oxygen and pulse have fallen too low. We have to put him on ventilator. Need your signature for the same,' replied the doctor.

Varun immediately signed the consent form. He called Rohan and informed him the same. At that moment they did not tell Zainab anything, not wanting to disturb her further. Zainab reached the hospital by evening, Varun stayed back to keep her company and that's when he told her about Shoaib being on life support. She sobbed through the evening, helplessly sitting outside the hospital, she feared the worst. They were about to leave for home at night when the doctor called Varun again.

'Please call Mr. Shoaib's wife,' said the doctor.

'Why? What happened?' He asked, extremely worried.

'We don't think he will make it through the night. I'm sorry,' said the doctor.

Varun dropped his phone in shock and sat down in his chair. He held his face in his hands and broke down.

'What happened Varun tell me. Is Shoaib okay?' asked Zainab.

Varun was unable to speak, he just nodded sideways to reply. Zainab broke down as well.

They went up to the ward and waited outside. After a couple of hours, the doctor came out of the ward.

'I'm sorry, he is no more,' said the doctor. Zainab and Varun could not stop crying.

'May I see him one last time?' asked Zainab.

'Sorry,' said the doctor. 'As per Covid norms, we can neither hand over the body to you nor are you allowed to enter the ward.'

Zainab could not bear the shock and passed out.

'Quickly, rush her to the non-Covid emergency department!' instructed the doctor.

While she recovered there, Varun and Rohan took care of the formalities and settled the hospital bill.

Life would never be the same for any of them. Zainab had lost her husband and the guys lost a dear friend. A couple of months passed by, and the lockdown was eased a little. Movement between districts was allowed and Joseph drove back to Mumbai. All the friends gathered at Varun's place since they had not met in a long time. Shoaib's loss was too much for them to bear. It was hard for them to accept their dear friend was no more. But such is life, it must go on. Varun's wife served them tea and snacks.

'How are you doing now?' Varun asked Rahul.

'I still feel weak. It's been 2 months, but I still haven't fully recovered. Damn these Chinese! But yes, testing early is what saved me. I only wish Shoaib had not hidden his health status from us,' said Rahul and sighed. It was followed by a couple of minutes of silence.

'Fear plays games with the mind. More than Covid getting to his lungs, I think it was fear getting to his mind that got the better of him,' said Varun. 'Anyways what's done is done. I'm sure he is in a better place. May he rest in peace.'

'Amen,' said all of them together.

Those were really dark days. This was the story of many. Some succumbed to fear, like Shoaib did. Some were alert and aware and managed to survive, like Rahul did. Then there were the courageous few, like Varun, who went beyond the ordinary to risk their own lives to help others. Those who survived, learnt an important lesson in gratitude. You cannot take a single day for granted. Being alive is enough to be grateful and to be happy because many a young men and women did not make it through the pandemic.

The Inner Awakening

@Ramya V.

'Slow, slow. Now a little left and then straight, straight.'

Neelima was instructing her younger brother Avinash to drive. Avinash was holding the steering wheel with a slight tremble in his fingers that had already caught Neelima' s attention. Avinash shrugged a bit.

'How are you able to drive like a professional? This seems so tough to me.' Avinash sighed.

'You need practice, mister. Moreover, some patience.' Neelima smiled.

'Just by looking at Papa's handling, now you are comfortable in driving a tractor. To some extent it is unbelievable.'

'Hey! By any chance, don't open your big mouth in front of Ma or Papa. They aren't aware of my skills.'

While the siblings laughed over trying to drive a tractor in their paddy fields, their parents were busy in fixing Neelima's wedding.

'Are you sure about this alliance?' Pavithra questioned her husband for the nth time.

'Do you think without enquiring about the boy and his family,

I would have asked them to visit us tomorrow?' Pavithra's husband, Sanjeev Mishra replied sternly.

'Our daughter holds a degree in Chemistry. Even now if she wishes she can get a job as a teacher. But you say that boy, oh what is his name? Ah Kiran, right! He is a college dropout in the final year who is now having some travel business. How do you think this would work?'

It was evident that Pavithra was not much interested, and it would take a while for Sanjeev to convince her, especially when he had already given his word for Kiran's family to come over to their house the next day.

'Kiran's family has been into business for over three decades. It was because of Kiran's intelligence that they now own two new lorries as initially, they managed only mini trucks. We should be lucky to have such a son-in-law in our family. Your daughter doesn't need to do a job and she will be the one who will give salary to the workers.' Sanjeev continued his praise.

Pavithra finally gave in, and so did Neelima. The wedding took place in a grand fashion, as almost every household of the village was present to bless the couple. Pavithra and Sanjeev were overwhelmed with joy at seeing their only daughter settled in her new home. Little did they know at that time that fate had other plans.

Neelima was happy with the love and affection offered by Kiran. Within a few months of their marriage, her in-laws moved to the neighbouring town to stay with Kiran's elder sister, who announced the good news of her pregnancy after eight years of married life. Kiran's parents considered Neelima to be a lucky charm and showered heaps of praises on her.

Kiran's office was a big room that was at the front of their house from where he managed his business. Mostly it involved booking contracts for delivering goods to the neighbouring villages and ensuring every day the delivery was on time. Neelima always felt so proud of her husband when she watched him handle any situation with ease, be it the differences between the drivers or the shop owners who urged for faster deliveries.

That morning, Neelima was busy in her routine, preparing lunch when she heard Kiran's voice, so loud that she could hear him in the kitchen which was unusual. Kitchen was at the back of the house. Quickly, she stopped her chopping work and hurried to the front.

'Listen to me first, Sir, please! There will not be any delay, I will come myself. Have I ever let you down?' Kiran was arguing over the phone. It was the first time Neelima saw him in such an agitated mood and confused state. Her eyes glanced around to see if she was able to deduce what the situation was. By then Kiran was done talking and sat in the chair to sip some water.

Neelima kept looking at him to open up.

'The government has announced a lockdown for twenty-one days. Do you remember we saw in the news for the past few days that some kind of virus is spreading all over the world? It is now almost a pandemic, and everyone has been told to stay at home. Our regular drivers have informed me they will not join duty considering the risk factor. We have signed contracts with our regular customers for two years. How will I manage? For essential travelling, the government is issuing a special permit. I told them I will get it soon, but no one is ready for travel.' With beads of sweat on his forehead, Kiran spilled his heart and Neelima understood his issue.

By then Chinnu, Kiran's assistant, came running with a slip that was required for the travel as the commodities they delivered were termed under essentials.

'I am starting now. Don't wait for me and have food on time.

I will be back by night.' Without waiting for Neelima's response, he rushed out with the papers to his truck and drove past in a flash.

Slowly, things changed. She cooked for both, but many days she had to eat alone and a few times she skipped cooking. Day or night, she never knew when Kiran would be home. Like dark clouds, days went by, and Neelima felt all would be over within a month. Only later she realised that it would never be over. The routine of cleaning anything bought, be it groceries or vegetables was now the 'new normal', amongst other things like sanitizing and masking. She took extreme care to wash them. Being at home for the entire day unknowingly she washed her hands' plenty of times. She was worried about Kiran and hoped he too was following the protocols correctly.

One night he reached home late, almost by twelve o' clock, feeling tired and fatigued. The next morning Kiran was running on high fever.

'Please rest today. I wanted to talk to you for a long time. Why can't we just return the advance payment and cancel the contracts? Do you even realise how much you are toiling? We have enough savings to last for years. You yourself have told me this. Then what is the need to burden your health so much? See you have lost three kgs in the past couple of months. You haven't spoken to anyone in our family. They miss—' before she even completed Kiran interrupted her with a rush.

'Can you keep quiet? It is not what it looks like. A few years ago, my sister's husband suffered a significant loss in his business, and I pledged the trucks to help him settle his debts. No one knows, not even my sister. I couldn't repay as the interests were huge and at that time, I really did not have an option. If I don't pay the interest even for a month, the next day you can expect unruly thugs lined up in front of our house demanding money, speaking in cuss words that you wouldn't have even heard of.'

Neelima's heart raced hearing every word. She felt Kiran could have shared the news a little early and not when they were in a critical crisis. Giving him pills for temperature, Neelima told Kiran to rest. After three days since he still had high fever, the local doctor insisted on him getting tested for Covid-19.

The next day they were shocked to see the result as positive. Neelima felt her world was already crumbling before her eyes. She needed help but it was impossible for her parents or in-laws to travel at this time. Every day the COVID affected cases only seemed to keep on rising, creating panic. Since Kiran's condition worsened, he was admitted to the hospital. Neelima struggled travelling to hospital and home. After twenty days, Kiran was back home. But he was too weak to even walk.

The nightmare came true as the people from whom Kiran borrowed money threatened to take away his vehicles. Neelima pleaded with them.

'Sir, please just give us one month. I promise to repay the interest of last month as well.'

Her tears and pleading words bought them some time. She can pawn her jewellery and pay money for 3 to 4 months. Then? Would Kiran be able to manage? Their workers refused to come back. This was survival in the long run and Neelima decided to take things in her own hands. With Chinnu's help she was able to drive the mini trucks. Though the number of trips would increase she was determined to ride them. Kiran did not favour her decision but knew there was no other option.

Initially, Neelima was reluctant about driving the lorry. Maybe its hugeness disturbed her confidence. But if she was able to do it, it could result in a lot of savings considering the hike in the fuel prices and the time taken for each trip. Chinnu understood her fears and encouraged her to try.

'*Didi*! (Sister) I believe you are truly talented. I am sure you can drive this one too. Handling the steering is the priority. Let us try driving in the night. If you are comfortable, we can try in the daylight. I will guide you.'

Chinnu's concern reminded her of Avinash, who had been her energy booster from their childhood. Listening to Chinnu's advice she decided to give it a try.

It was late night and Kiran was fast asleep. Neelima neared the big bird. She got in and ignited it to life. It roared like a lion. Chinnu was seated beside her. He carefully instructed her and then she began to get control of the steering. After getting onto the road, Neelima felt a bit relaxed as she drove slowly. Switching gears, she now was driving smoothly. They returned home after a while. Every night she continued her lessons and soon she was effortlessly driving the giant eagle.

She hesitated to inform Kiran about it as she was sceptical as to how he would react. But Chinnu insisted that Kiran would only be happy to hear this huge news. Half-heartedly, she informed Kiran. She thought he would yell at her but instead he remained calm which worried her even more.

'Neelima! I am so proud of you. When you first told me, that you were driving the trucks yourself I admit, it just angered me. Your security and safety were my primary concern. And I had to let you do this because of our situation. After seeing your confidence and determination I am truly overwhelmed with joy to have such a blessed wife in my life. It is in tough times we understand who we really are. You were brave all the while. You never gave up. We are reading in newspapers how many lives were affected due to this pandemic. You are one among the strong ones who stood firm. Not only that, but you also held me up with your courage. Without you I would have crumbled. I am sure you will be a role model to many in our village.' With a few drops of tears escaping from his eyes Kiran hugged Neelima closely.

She couldn't believe what she was hearing. His words made her to think hard and it was a moment of self-realisation for her. It is true! At hard times we fall, how we stand up again and again, fighting every moment defines one's nature. She secretly thanked the pandemic for making her understand herself even better.

'Neelima!'

Her reverie was disturbed by his words.

'Now you are also one of the partners in our business. So, any decision taken will have your opinion as well.' Kiran smiled. She blushed and buried herself in his arms.

Love During Quarantine

@ Pavan Revannavar

12th March 2020

I came home for the *Holi* (an Indian festival of colours) weekend. It's been eight months now, but the weekend hasn't ended. The world went in quarantine. It's been months and months now. At the start, it was all cool, beautiful, and smooth. A month passed and boredom started settling in. What next? There was no answer to this question at all. I was spending hours on social media, just scrolling and surfing.

I knew that the phenomenon of meeting people online existed but had hardly experienced it till this quarantine happened. That day, when I was going through a post on Instagram, I saw a comment on that post which hit me so hard that I couldn't resist replying to it. I replied to that comment and so, started a conversation. Somehow, something touched my heart about that post; it felt real, not fake. In a world full of filters and fake blandishments she felt real, and this is how she introduced herself without even saying anything. Hence started a new chapter of talking to a stranger.

Then I knew that I hardly knew myself, too. It felt great telling her everything that made me happy and about any things that often made me sad. Soon, we shifted from comments, which everyone could read to DMs (Direct messages). We talked of spending time in quarantine, and how we wished life went back to being as it was during the pre-covid days. We were from different cities, in fact from different corners of the country. I am from South India, and she is from North. Different cultures, different people, and also different perspectives. As we talked more and got to know each other, we realised we had chosen very different career paths. She was doing psychology and I was an engineer.

An engineer and a phycologist don't sound that great together. Yet, we gelled very well, and we became online friends as we spoke to each other for hours and more. Conversation shifted from texts to calls and from calls to video calls. We told each other the pettiest of things, like why she likes her coffee strong and why I like my chai without the *adrak* (ginger). Favourite music, food, movies, shows and everything else under the sun was discussed and analysed threadbare. Yes, we both were aware that we may not ever meet and there were very few chances of our paths ever crossing. This reality check was always there—unspoken, unacknowledged but intruding conspicuously.

We knew that we had become the best of friends from being random strangers. It feels good when someone likes you without even seeing you physically even once. In a world where people judge you for each and every bit of whatever you do, it's tough to find people who understand you and judge less. I felt truly blessed to have found her during the worst phase of my life, quarantined at home and nothing much to do. Time passed swiftly, with her to converse with every day. We became each other's quarantine partners and made sure we never got bored and kept our spirits up. Jokes exchanged, incidents laughed over, family cribbing sessions kept us going for most part. I felt that I had finally found something that I had always been looking for— a friend who listens, suggests some solutions to problems and says things gently without hurting.

Months passed, seasons changed, summers went, monsoons happened yet the pandemic was still there. Sitting cooped up inside the house was nerve wracking to say the least, and the only solace was my conversations with my quarantine friend.

People adapted and started to learn how to live with a pandemic. As everyone had started getting used to this 'new normal', quarantine came to an end. Things opened up, offices became offline again, the hustle bustle started with the markets opening, and roads were alive again with vehicular traffic.

But a major thing was happening close by, too. We realised our feelings for each other, that we were really into each other. Virtual was all good until we felt the urge of seeing each other physically and in front of each other. There were so many pictures we had seen of each other, that now the need to see each other had become a topmost priority for both of us.

Now, we came to a realisation that the paths we thought we would never cross, wouldn't happen until we made it happen. So now, after too many calculations about how and when, I decided to take matters in my hands and go and visit her. Niggling doubts like her family judging me, her disappointment on seeing me (maybe) were brushed under the carpet and I took a decisive step.

Finally, we took the big step.

I was excited, nervous, anxious, and what-not. But what buoyed my confidence was that she, too, was equally nervous. I remember her asking me in what dress I would like to see her, what colour would suit her, and hope things would turn out good for us, both. I reassured her things would turn out fine, though I, too, was a nervous wreck from inside.

Anyways, all of this didn't make me any less excited about meeting her. At last, now when I have booked tickets to Lucknow after so much back and forth in my mind. Now, Lucknow is a place which is going to show my new world to me. She has lined up my every minute with some activity or another. She plans to show me everything that she had told me about her city. She has planned our time together with lots of love and care. She has planned our first date to the T. Let's see how it all goes after this.

I am at the airport right now writing this story, from where she is supposed to pick me up and she is late already, for which she has apologised profusely. Wish me luck. The world said that 2020 bought too many disasters and also some wonderful surprises. I agree; quarantine was a disaster, but it did bring me my soulmate—a wonderful surprise when I was least expecting it and I am loving it.

Homecoming

@Vasudha Kapoor Duggal

Latha woke up with a start. Was it the bell? Yes, the bell had been ringing. It was 8 a.m. She jolted out of bed and quickly walked to open the main door. There was an Amazon delivery.

She took the package and went back to her bed. Yawning, she sat on her bed contemplating her day's work plan—the spreadsheet needed to be completed before the 3p.m. con-call. Shouldn't take more than a couple of hours. 70% she had already completed earlier.

It had been six months since she moved to this rented tiny flat in the heart of Bangalore, about fifteen kilometres from her parents sprawling house. Though her parents were not too happy about this, they had given in to her insistence. Since college, Latha wanted to live on her own, just like some of her friends. So impressed was she by their independent lifestyle and their exciting tales, that she had secretly determined she would move out once she had a stable job.

After her biotechnology degree, she had been working for two years and this desire to live alone kept gnawing at her. It wasn't easy convincing her parents. *Why? What's the need? You have all comfort here, you don't have to worry about housework, everything is smooth sailing on auto pilot, you can live a carefree happy life, it's not safe alone etc.*

Latha was adamant. Why should she have problems? Her friends were living alone for many years and were very content. After all, she was a 24-year-old adult and wanted to live with no *'toka-taki'* (interference)—no questioning about her whereabouts, her outings, or time limits to her outings. Besides, she wanted to experience living on her own, running her own house, cooking her own meals.

She was also irritated about her mother's disapproval of her growing friendship with Sam and that her mom came out with different objections every time Latha went out with him.

'Please stop judging and let us be. What's important is that I like him,' Latha would retort.

She had loved her little den. The first couple of months, she was living her dream as she went about setting up the place—decorating it, stocking the little fridge with her choicest food, and generally loitering around the place contentedly. She had found a maid who came in the mornings to do her cooking and housework. Her friends dropped in on weekends and they all chilled together. Her place became the default hangout place for all. She got to spend so much more time with Sam without the probing eyes of her mother. No wonder kids in the West moved out of their parent's place once they were of age. Made full sense.

Latha had been going steady with Sam for more than a year. He used to work in the same company before he quit to start his own venture. She was drawn to him not just because he was attractive, but because of his eloquence. He had the gift of the gab, which when coated by his sense of humour, impressed all and sundry. After moving out of her parents' place, they met more frequently.

In the third month of her stay, there were some plumbing issues in the bathroom. Getting hold of a plumber and having him fix the problem took a good three days which were a bit challenging for her. She had to call off the small party they had planned to celebrate a friend's promotion. After all, there was only one bathroom. Another irritant was the maid who came early at 6.30 am, interrupting her sleep. She had to be up to let her in, no matter how late she had slept. And in her drowsy state, she often forgot the things she needed the maid to do, thus ending up doing them herself. No amount of coaxing made the maid change her timing and it wasn't easy to find another one.

And after five months of her stay, the pandemic struck, and lockdown happened. Working from home was a pleasant change. The maid stopped coming which meant Latha could sleep till late and quickly log in for work without even getting ready. The downside was she had to fend for her meals herself and do all the housework. There were times when she didn't get a breather from work and couldn't get to eat till late afternoon. That's when she missed home. Of course, her mother fretted about this no end.

'If only you had listened to me and not moved out,' she moaned, 'you wouldn't be famished every day like this. *Arre* (hey), after marriage, all this would have anyway befallen you.'

'Chill, *Ma*, let's look at the positive side—maybe this will help me lose some weight,' countered Latha.

'And listen Latha, please don't eat outside food. You just never know from where the virus creeps in!'

In the weekends that followed, though she got to sleep to her heart's content, there was a whole lot of housework to be done. She spent more time coping with the chores than pursuing her reading or watching OTT series.

She had not met her friends or Sam for four weeks now. Yes, it was getting lonely. That night while chatting with Sam on the phone, she was taken aback when Sam proposed to her. Much as they liked each other, she was not expecting this. Not at this time. Not like this. It was too sudden. She hadn't thought about this, and she needed time.

Sam was definitely a very likable person. Armed with a Management from FMS, Delhi, he had started his own business in the manufacturing and supply of pharmaceutical instruments and devices, which had taken off pretty well. And according to him, the pandemic had made the prospects even more promising for the pharmaceutical industry.

Though undecided, she felt light and upbeat. She had never met his family who lived in Goa. But what was important was that she enjoyed his company, and they could chat non-stop for hours. *Didn't they say marry a person with whom you could talk to? With whom you could have healthy no holds barred conversations? Wasn't that supposed to be one of the key ingredients of a successful marriage?* So, one check box ticked. Academic credentials ticked. Career prospects ticked. Religion didn't matter. Not to her, but it could be of concern to her parents that their prospective son-in-law was a Christian. But she could handle them. The important thing was that they liked and enjoyed each other's company.

Humming, she freshened up, quickly made some coffee, and logged into her laptop. The spreadsheet needed full attention before the *con-call* in the afternoon.

A week passed by, and Sam didn't pursue the topic. Guess he was respecting her need for time to think. Nice of him, she mused.

Latha was by now, seeped with the increasing office work and meetings. Work pressure was building up and with no time limits. At least, when she went to the office, she was free by 6 PM and then had her own free time. Now, work was assigned anytime and with crazy deadlines. She ended up working till late evenings. Adding to this pressure was the cooking she needed to do. How much Maggi and sandwiches could she have! She yearned for proper meals.

And then, just like that, Sam came up with his so-called bright idea. Why doesn't he move in with her? That way they could manage the housework together and even get to know each other better.

'What! You mean live-in? No, no, that's not done. I'll be ostracised from my community. And my parents will disown me,' said Latha.

'Come on Latha. How will your parents and community know? And isn't this the best way to know a person well, before taking the plunge in today's age?'

Latha was hesitant.

'Look, you have no reason to worry. I'll sleep in the living room. If that's what's worrying you. But we'll get to spend so much time together.'

So once there was some relaxation in the lockdown, one Saturday—Sam was at the door, suitcase in hand. Latha didn't know how to react. Still hesitant, and a bit nervous, she let him in. That day, they just chilled, glued to Netflix together. Sam ordered food assuring that the house drill would start from the following day.

And sure enough, Sunday saw the two of them giving the flat a new shine. While Sam did the cleaning, Latha cooked 3-4 dishes in large quantities to last the next couple of days. She washed the clothes and the bedsheets while he dried them all. Sam put on some music and in between their chores, they danced and twirled merrily.

Two months went by cheerfully. The housework that was weighing heavy on Latha's shoulders was lightened by Sam's helping hand. Between themselves they managed their office work as well all housework. Life was good. Latha started appreciating Sam's hands-on helping approach in just about every aspect of house-care. She discovered a good cook in him. But what she loved the most was the fact that he had absolutely no misogynistic traits in him, something she had seen closely and resented, in her father and uncles. Even when they had their arguments, he was willing to hear her perspective with an open mind and was always cool and willing to compromise amicably.

She loved him even more. She had made up her mind. This was going to be her man. This was the person she wanted to spend her life with.

But these happy two months soon came to an end when Sam had to rush to Goa as his father had tested positive and was hospitalised.

Latha was once again alone. With office pressure, she could not cope with all the chores without a maid. She struggled a good ten days amidst all the pressures all alone. She missed home cooked food. She wanted warm people around her. She wanted someone to talk to. She missed her family and the warmth of her parents' care. Loneliness gripped Latha.

Latha called her mother that evening and was almost in tears as she shared her ordeals and feelings.

'Don't worry, I'm sending Vish to bring you back home. Just pack your essentials. Your remaining stuff can come later in the weekend,' quipped her mother.

That very night, her brother Vish, came to pick her up. She was already packed and ready when he came.

And what a welcome she got from her family when she got home!

The next few days Latha devoured her favourite dishes cooked by her mother. Nothing like home food. Nothing like getting the best food without having to cook yourself. Gosh! What she had been missing.

Every day after dinner, they played carrom, chatted and watched TV together. She was now liking this far better than her days living alone on her own. One does not realise the little mercies of life until one actually experiences living without them. How much gets taken care of by one's parents and family, is something she now valued. Staying alone was fun, but for a limited period. Nothing like having your loving family around. This was her new awakening.

When Sam called, she sensed his relief when he informed that his father was stable and recovering well. He too could easily make out how relieved she was, back home amidst family.

Sam's father was discharged after a week and Sam returned to Bangalore soon after. They decided they needed to formally introduce each other to their families. She met his family members over a zoom call. Sam had already apprised them about her.

She too had spoken to her family about his proposal. He started visiting her at home as going out while the virus was still lurking was not an option yet. As her parents got to know him better, all their reservation lost steam. It was clearly evident they were impressed by him and enjoyed his sense of humour.

Sam and Latha decided to have a small wedding at Sam's Goa home in the coming winter. Happiness and excitement writ large on everyone's faces. There was so much to look forward to, so much to plan and shop. Sam was expecting to get possession of his flat by October, which needed to be done up so they could move in there after the wedding.

'Do you now appreciate what a good proposition I had made when I asked to move in? Didn't it help you make up your mind?'

asked Sam.

'It sure did. And I saw your point, that's why I agreed! So, some credit goes to me too,' winked Latha.

In fact, living away in that small house in the pandemic, brought in many realisations and taught her many life lessons. She shuddered as she remembered the three days of fever and body ache that she went through with no one to tend to her and no one to talk to. She understood what it was to be lonely for the first time in her life. It helped her realise the joys and comfort of living with family. And now she wanted to enjoy the entire time, till she got married, amidst her loving family.

Acceptance is Bliss Sometimes!

@Pooja Mandla

Flashes of vivid images flow through my heart,
Flickering memories of non-pandemic past.
When life was free like a bird flying high,
Wandering across the pink morning sky.
Sans any encompassing fear of tiny virus,
Now for such days, we are desirous.
When meeting friends, family, and socialising wasn't having restrictions,
Public transport, dining out and holidaying didn't have limitations.
But complaining all the time can make our life shabby,
Counting our blessings would make us happy.
Acceptance to the new normal is the need of the hour,
Masks and gloves are must things no matter who we are.
Creating a routine that can give some sense of normalcy,
Online Gym and getting creative can show some positivity.
As it's a privilege to be alive and healthy these days,
It's better to keep all the negativity at bay.
Absurd it is to complain that rose bushes are full of thorns,
Accept the new normal, be happy that the thorns still have roses that are yours!

Quarantine or Quarrel Time?

@Uma Divgi

Disclaimer: This my 'aap beeti' (my memoirs).
Read on at your own risk!

Uff! (Oh!) Is this Quarantine or is it Quarrel Time? I completely agree with the old saying 'distance makes the heart grow fonder' but then also, I want to add 'close proximity makes the heart grow distant'.

March 2020, Covid struck and surrounded us with uncertainty, doubt, and most of all—fear. It began its ruthless attack on us innocent, unsuspecting beings. It took away our freedom, took away our confidence and left millions in utter misery, and so many others helpless.

A tsunami of unknown fears enveloped the world over. Anxiety, sadness, hatred—a mixed bag of varied emotions, leaving even our saviours, our doctors confused.

Covid creeped in stealthily into the nearby cities and towns. Then it struck our own neighbourhood and then right below our noses, our friends, and neighbours—though we were all masked and took the required precautions, it was still very frightening.

Many a friend experienced the wrath but fought it bravely and emerged victorious, while some unfortunately succumbed. Grieving took another dimension altogether—imagine with no near and dear ones to even console or lend a shoulder to cry on or even a compassionate hug. Could there be a worse punishment?

The flipside of this covid invasion during the first lockdown was the sudden joy of unexpected holidays, 'Now I'll get more time to fulfil the new year resolutions, do some renovations, read, paint, join online singing class, learn stitching & basically dive into any and every hobby I had yearned to do since my childhood.' I thought to myself.

But of course, cooking took most of my time and anyways—it was priority number one. Experimenting with different cuisines and recipes, I'm sure everyone—irrespective of gender has an album of 'Lockdown Dishes'. Food being the highlight of most homes, right from healthy eating, and heavy diets. With nothing much to do, exercise also brought about a major lifestyle change.

Along with indulging our food cravings, we took to watching *OTT* web series and movies with a vengeance, something for which till now we had no time for—what with our busy schedules and long hours. A frantic exchange of who's watched what and recommendations for new stuff ensued, aided with a generous dollop of WhatsApp chats.

Soon, it too lost its charm when horrifying stories of the pandemic and its fallout flashed across our TV screens. The migrants' long walk home, people losing their jobs, small businesses closing down got us depressed and worrying about what was coming next.

Work-From-Home, a not so common phrase for us in India till then, took on a new meaning. No office hours meant the work continued all day long, at the mercy of the powers above—and clocking in the required amount of office time along with household chores was a nightmarish experience, to say the least.

To make things worse, here was I, who in spite of my better judgement—took my husband's advice to retire early just so we could make hay while the sun shines; by that I mean go globetrotting while the body's bits and pieces were still intact and functioning—that, by the way, was his argument.

So happily, husband and I hung our spurs, so to say and wore our walking shoes—all ready—bags packed, itinerary made, all set to tick off destinations off the bucket list and voila! Yes, you guessed it—we got struck by the dampener. So, travelling anywhere, let alone by our bucket list was out, a complete washout.

By now coping with life and its disappointments kept growing persistently from days to weeks to months. Soon another realisation dawned on us that although we have dwelled in one house since our marriage; but for the past couple of decades, we were busy in our own respective lives of work, school, children, exams, in-laws, parents, new friends, new hobbies—we were basically in a bubble of our own and enjoying our own space.

But now, with both locked down at home, we were now in each other's hair (my tresses of course). Daily, 24/7, ouch! And if it hadn't been for the height difference (he is like Jack's Beanstalk to my Rapunzel) we would have been looking at each other eye to eye. So yes, we were on a roller coaster ride together, the only difference being we were not shouting with mirth but with anger. Mahabharata the epic was being played out again—and of course, you guessed it—who was the kaurava here. But I won't delve into the nitty-gritties as we all go through our own unique flavours of fights.

Finally, my *sole* mate (remember the walking shoes bit?) decided he needed to relate to something unconditional, loyal, unanswerable to kind of partner for life. Basically, he desperately wanted a pet preferably a four legged one, even a cow would have done, but his bitter half (Remember me?) is petrified of the bow-wows and imagining keeping a cow still gives me the heebie-jeebies.

But a pet we had to have to neutralise the war like situation. So, the man of the house decided on nothing less than a talking bird and now we are the proud bird parents of little Koko—an African Grey Parrot, registered and totally ours, a legal nine-month-old, who is a sheer delight to have around.

Koko is equal to Royalty—he lives in a spacious, well protected barred cage, furnished with a variety of different perches with different textures to keep his soles healthy. He has room service with the choicest of delicacies right from exotic dragon fruit, big fat red Australian grapes and kiwis to name a few and veggies like broccoli, peas, corn, with brown rice, if you please.

The seeds right from chia, hemp to pomegranate keeps Koko happy—not to miss the dry crushed worms twice a week mixed with his formula in coconut water. Koko is a free bird and is out of the cage most of the time perched on his daddy's shoulder. Greys are normally one-man loyalist, so he is a total daddy's baby, and our dad couldn't be happier. After-all that's what he wanted—unconditional love and loyalty. He derives the greatest pleasure when little Koko hops off the tall broad shoulders on to the sofa, climbs down, struts on the table in between, walks up to the unsuspecting mother, i.e., me, and ouch! Pecks hard enough (without any reason) to make me jump out of my skin. It's as if Koko can read my sole—err soul mates' mind, by the delightful look that crosses his face. He preens like a proud parent when

Koko looks at him for approval! Oh yes exactly that, I am sure he must be ever thankful to Koko for his unconditional support. He has finally found a partner that he had always wanted.

So now the happy times are back again—everyone is happy in these covid times! Peace has been finally restored at the homestead. Each to his own, once again, with a small skirmish here or there. Now that we are walking into the third year of the good (really?), the bad, the ugly, we are well prepared to face the worst.

PS: My sources tell me that we may now be well past covid, what with the vaccine out, and herd immunity leaping and spreading.

Amen to that.

PPS: In case you are wondering, Koko stays!

Transformed in Quarantine

@Shirley Verghese

The pandemic came as an unbelievable shock for people across the globe. It is one thing to be enthralled by extreme unimaginable situations in sci-fi novels, portrayed in films like (Contagion, Carriers, Virus, to name a few) or read about it in contemporary literature (e.g., 'Blindness' by Jose Saramago, 'The end of October' by Lawrence Wright, 'The Great Believers' by Rebecca Makkai) or to trace the genesis of such world catastrophes; and a totally different scene for a person in today's time to visualise being alive in an excruciating day to day ordeal of this unforeseen magnitude that swept across humanity from east to west, with no respite. The manner of its appearance and taking over was unpredictable. It gave no time to find remedies nor attempt trials for alternative treatments. There was no premonition that the final detrimental blow was going to be so vicious and irrevocable.

It is true that irony dies a thousand deaths when history repeats itself even in the appearance of uninvited viruses every hundred year or so! We had *The Great Spanish Flu* of 1918 which was a pandemic and *the Bombay Flu* around 1917. An epidemic had wiped out a pre-historic village in Northeast China (the site is called Hamin Mangha), some 5000 years ago. With poor development of medicines, humanity was ravaged time and again by the deadly Plague, caused by fleas affecting rodents. *The Plague of Athens* in 430 B.C., probably caused by Typhoid or Ebola virus, broke out after the relentless war between Athens and Sparta, which lasted for five years. Presumably, the smallpox virus was brought back by Roman soldiers returning from Sparta with their spoils of victory! It was known as the *Antonine Plague* (A.D. 165-180), which finally brought down the magnificent Roman Empire under its best Emperor Marcus Aurelius.

This was followed by the *Cyprian Plague* (A.D. 250-271) and the *Justiman Plague* (A.D. 541-542) that destroyed the Byzantine Empire with Bubonic Plague. *The Black Death* (1346-1353) travelled from Asia to Europe leaving a trail of devastation that wiped out half of Europe's population. People had to be buried in mass graves and it changed the course of Europe's labour force, which since then was hard to find. It led to technological innovations and the beginning of the industrial revolution. The *Cocoliztli Epidemic* (1545-1548) killed 15 million inhabitants of Mexico and Central America caused by a subspecies of the Salmonella, causing haemorrhagic enteric fever, which is a health threat till date. The 16th century saw a series of *American Plague* brought by European Explorers that wiped out 90% of the indigenous American population in North and South America.

In 1665-1666, *The Great Plague of London* followed the Black Death and half of the population in and around London vanished. It happened again in France (1720-1723) with the docking of a ship "Grand Saint Antoine" in Marseille, carrying cargo from the Eastern Mediterranean countries. *The Russian Plague* of 1770-1772 saw public outcries to quarantine, which then erupted in violence. An Archbishop who did not encourage crowds from gathering for worship was murdered. Even the queen Catherine the Great, could do nothing to restore order where a million citizens died. *The Yellow Fever epidemic* of 1793 in Philadelphia, spread by mosquitoes in the hot humid months, saw a lot of deaths. The negro population was entrusted with nursing the whites, as they were believed to be resistant to the deadly fever.

The precursor to our present pandemic can be compared with the *Spanish Flu* of 1918-20, where 500 million people died as a direct consequence of the World War I. Interestingly, the name is a misnomer, since the disease did not actually start in Spain, but since they were the ones who first published early accounts of the illness, the name stuck. The *Asian bird Flu* first came up in 1957-58 and a few times later. The *AIDs epidemic* took over the world in 1980 claiming 35 million lives and stays a threat even today. Fortunately, medications to prevent death by *Human Immunodeficiency Virus (HIV)* have since been working to save lives. *The H1N1 Swine Flu* was another pandemic in 2009-2010 that originated in Mexico before spreading worldwide. A vaccine has been developed to combat this fatal sickness affecting children and young people.

There is one great learning through this experience down the ages, which has been conveniently forgotten. Humanity will definitely have to pay the price for their omissions and commissions with precious lives without warning. Living in harmony with nature, with love and brotherhood rather than wars and strife is perhaps the only solution. A lesson yet to be learned and lived by.

Reflecting upon the past two years of the quarantine days, my personal encounter was pretty uneventful. We were spared the experience of becoming infected, were able to get vaccinated in time and strictly followed the norms for safety and precautions. But there were many aspects that I became sensitised to. We were just back from a quick trip to our hometown in Kerala around March 14th when the lockdown was put in effect from the 21st of March 2020. The most shocking impact was taking on the chores of housemaids, drivers, cleaning staff and cooks for an indefinite period. It was a staggering reality as no one was allowed to step out of their houses. The days were endless, often with unfinished work on hand and shortcuts (which we perhaps did not grant them) to quickly finish off the jobs. Physical stamina and will power, both were in short supply.

Initially, the sub-staff were glad for the unexpected break of paid holidays, but after a while even they missed their outing and work. They begged to come back, by then we had rewired our head and body to function as per need. There was great pride in sweeping and swabbing floors, dusting windows, doors, frames, furniture that looked spotless and shining after hours of sweet labour. However, the chores never ceased. Wading through washing utensils, drying clothes, chopping vegetables, peeling garlic, ginger, scraping coconut, kneading dough, rolling out round *chapattis* (Indian flattened breads)—I just could not step out of the kitchen till 2 p.m. The timetable for breakfast, lunch and dinner got compromised and there were no complains! We learned to sincerely appreciate the contributions of our tireless staff.

The first two months were the most difficult. We had to figure out how to organise supplies of groceries and essential food items, which took longer than usual to procure from shops or online stores. I had not ventured out of the house, nor seen anyone in the neighbourhood. It became claustrophobic. Thankfully, the phones and television were a medium that kept us connected. However, the news one heard of situations in different parts of the world and in our own country was alarming. Scenes of suffering people, shortage of oxygen and medicines, overflowing hospitals, empty streets and finally the exodus of the afflicted jobless migrant working classes from the big cities to the villages of Bihar, Orissa and Bengal was depressing. The mood was sombre, and the heart was always heavy. The stories of misery, death, and lack of money in the hands of people made us feel guilty sitting comfortably at our homes, grateful for small mercies of our life, with more empathy and concern for those who bore the brunt of the have nots.

Looking around at the hardship experienced by ordinary people was heart-wrenching. Small businesses and shops had to shut down. There were no activities that could generate income that could reach the homes and hearth of the lower middle class and poorer working community. It affected their dignity to be reduced to helplessness. By and large, children from all denominations missed proper schooling. They were losing their concentration span and the enthusiasm for learning by looking onto small phones or TV screens for long hours for lessons. In small villages, there would be 10-12 children cramped around one 15-inch TV screen for online lessons. The more affluent kids learned to remain unruly, forfeiting the need for discipline in a social setup. Often, they attended class without proper grooming, not wearing school uniforms, switching off video mode so that they are not seen by others.

The emotional disturbance of confining to small spaces, not meeting people, not being able to give and take a warm hug, masking for hours and social distancing had its toll on everyone, young and old. It was painful to train little babies and children to wear masks, gloves and sanitise their little hands. So many restrictions for sitting and playing with friends. To get familiar with long distance family and relatives through the phones, laptops and iPad for the kids was perhaps puzzling. Perhaps, they too seem to appear like one of the characters of the cartoons in familiar stories. One wonders if their tiny hearts would be able to love and find attachments that needs to be nurtured and sustained. I am still sceptical about the absence of expressing genuine affection in these long-distance virtual love and connections. This is the dynamics that exists between parents, children, and their grandchildren—who are reduced to a ritual meeting on weekly basis or so. How does one keep alive a sense of care, concern, and interest, when there is no physical presence or proximity?

There is a kind of unspeakable grief and sadness that overwhelms everyone in their hearts. Some are able to ignore that sense of gloom and keep diverting their attention with physical and mental activities. Nevertheless, heavy drops of gathering gloom underline the psyche till it becomes a cancerous cloud of melancholy. It tends to override the rational mind from holding on to reality and triggers unexpected patterns of behaviour and thought processes. Comparisons, ridiculous accusations, negative notions reduce the self-esteem needs of the affected person. Having endured these excruciating battles between sense and sensibility, I am able to spell this out today. Not that I have succeeded in being on top of it, for I often find myself flung around randomly between doubt and fear, love, and rejection, of being valued or let gone off. It is a terrible feeling. I, therefore, feel safer in this new bubble of isolation and detachment.

It has led to a new sense of indulgence, getting solace in this ostracised zone of loneliness and solitude. Something that was difficult and unimaginable initially has turned into a comforter in self-isolation. I for one, do enjoy the company of people having fun and laughter around me. But at the end of these two years, I feel more and more reticent. I find myself moving to places within me that were neglected so long. I was not inclined to meet anyone in particular. There was no enthusiasm nor excitement to dress up, to go somewhere, or eat out at a nice restaurant. I just wanted to be, in my new expanse of serenity.

'Main aur meri tanhayi.' Me and my solitude. I found a new friend in me.

It is perhaps the reason for my endless sleepless nights,

pondering about unanswered questions - knowing how it feels to be really afraid of darkness and then to shut my eyes, with my mind wide awake and walk through it holding out my hands to feel my way. I can empathise with those who suffer the hopelessness of terminal illness and how they meet every wakeful moment of life as their last breath. I began to appreciate every small and big thing that happened in my life. I also realised the futility of all the rat-races and pursuits that once took my time and attention. Like a track that remains intact, long after the races are done; I am here, with the same desires, wants, needs, and fears, then and now. The only difference being that I now know how to deal with each one of them. There are things that one can change and there are many to which we have to adapt, succumb and live with. Those are the most painful realisations that can be learned with a sense of objective detachment.

To find a meaning and purpose from these shambles, one must therefore be able to grasp the true essence of existence. Find the balance between expectations, desires, and possibilities. To be able to chart the course of this transient life span with our creative thoughts and actions that makes us feel joy and fulfilment, while we are around. There, I said it. Perhaps not as easy to make that happen, nevertheless if one could inspire to see that objective in our daily routine, our soul could soar sans our body. We must merge into the cycle of nature as the elements transit from one form to the other effortlessly. Sometimes as snowflakes, or raindrops or hailstones. Sometimes as whispering winds, as hot and vibrant flames of fire. At other times, flow gently in streams or swiftly in the rivers and or ride the wild waves of the seas. Or stay as witness for thousands of years, as a speck of sand, a boulder, or a gigantic mountain.

The Quarantine days have become a part of me and my pattern. It taught me patience, resilience, and courage. It makes me value love and bear compassion for humanity. It reminds me of the treasure of all the memories of wonderful people in my life and the exotic places that I have been to and enjoyed.

Existing Existence

@Nidhi H. Khasgiwale

Initially it was a preclusive measure,
Just another one of life's endeavours.

It got spine-chilling day by day,
Weakening was the captivating charisma of Bombay.

With not a soul on the streets,
The planet seemed so incomplete.

Days went by, I got more terrified,
Hearing of the earthlings who had recently died.

Wondering if this was just a lie,
I asked God, 'Why?'

I was aghast at the mention of the lockdown,
But pronto showed up Anne and the rest of Charlottetown.

Hogwarts, Agrabah & Green Gables,
How I yearned they weren't just portrayals.

Television and books became our only escape,
In both, Harry and Ron were awfully terrorised by Snape.

None of us could fathom that this was probably fate,
Who knows? Banner might've even gained some weight.

While some were hypnotised by the glamour of Archie,
I wondered, did Hardman actually think he could fire Harvey?

Dear Almighty, may this be just another fearsome dream,
Please work your necromancy, The Sorcerer Supreme.

We are, after all, nothing but mortals,
Will Daniels won't always be on the other side of those portals.

Gatherings took place through meetings on Zoom,
During history lectures the hero was good old, A.O. Hume.

Video-calls were made to our *Chachi & Chacha* (aunts and
uncles),
Hurray! Rafa has finally been overthrown by Sascha.

So many homo-sapiens were sinking in debt,
Your comebacks amused us, Princess Margaret.

It was futile to debate with the cosmos,
I just wanted to catch a flight to the Galapagos!

Drawing and painting were bliss for me,
It gave me a little positivity.

The world had come to a standstill,
Folks were falling dreadfully ill.

Out of the blue we became outlanders,
Wondering whether we could turn back the calendars.

We wished we could go back to when masks were not garments,
And were not confined to our blissful apartments.

All we can do is have faith that it will cease,
And eventually there will be the reign of peace.

A Bittersweet Lesson

@Uma Bokil

Pune, Maharashtra

This is a story that took place in almost every house over and across the world. This is a story that we all have been living, feeling, experiencing, and sharing—a story we will all remember; a story of revelations, and of renewing lost friendships and torn bonds.

It was an afternoon on 20th March 2020 when I strutted back home and plopped down heavily on the couch, a huge sigh of exhaustion leaving my lips. My grandmother was hospitalised, and I had been moving around within hospital walls amidst the threat of a global pandemic. That day, thankfully, she was coming home. It was a time when masks were not our uniform and every shop had run out of sanitisers.

The next day, every television was running and re-running the Prime Minister's address to the country. The nation would be under absolute lock and key from 22nd March 2020. No one was to step out of their houses. Of course, it was a problem for a lot of people who were stuck in another city due to work, or not actually home. But not for me.

I had been living a year or two of my life commuting to places within the city throughout the day, and only coming home to sleep under comforting sheets. Till that point, I had been denying the obvious—that I had gotten tired of it; frustrated, even. The national lockdown for one day had changed the way I had begun looking at my life—the one day I never thought I would need.

On the morning of 22nd March, I woke up feeling rested. My family was happily chirping and chatting, but at the back of every mind was one question—how does India look without people on its streets? It was a sight so unusual that I could hardly recognise the streets I would have otherwise identified on any other day. The drone showing images flew over and across the renowned, usually crowded Peth areas. That must have been the first time in twenty years that I actually got to see the roads in the Peth.

My family was cooking together, laughing, and sharing stories together—somewhere amidst all the wrongs happening in the world, something felt right. The carrom board was dusted and cleaned, and a treasure hunt ensued to find out the decks of cards whose existence had been forgotten. I wished then, just for a fleeting second—to be able to do this more often. How could I have known that my wish was about to be granted for the next four months?

After clusters of people filled up every nook and corner the following Monday, we were hit with a blow. The nation was put under lockdown for the next twenty-one days, with the exception of medical stores and extreme necessities. This would be later extended to three more months. My father and I divided the chores and got to work.

I was well aware that it was going to be tougher than I could foresee. My routine changed completely. I worried less about getting stuck in rush-hour traffic and worried more about helping Mom getting our meals ready on time. I had always thought of wanting to live by my own after a while, but I had never given this side of it a thought. To make matters worse (or better, I can say when I look back now), I broke my phone. For the next ninety days, I was going to be without it. I was devastated at first, but astoundingly, not for long.

I started being more in the present moment. Forget being, I was actually living every moment. I am an early bird, so waking up at seven in the morning and lazing around with my phone had switched to sipping the freshest cup of tea in the balcony and listening to the music of the birds. The time I used to spend scrolling through a mindless feed was replaced by books, my long-forgotten friends. The fragrance of old pages of books came back as I switched to the good old days of old-school reading.

I enjoyed reading and completed eight to ten books in a month and a half. I reconnected with the power of words. I eyed cooking with newly found respect, something which I would have scorned earlier. *Why should I tether myself to the kitchen?* I used to mock. But kitchen chores had taken a form of essential life skills in my eyes, something I realised I would need eventually for my own survival. My evenings were spent on the terrace, watching the sunset every day. I sang a little, wrote a little, laughed a little, and lived a lot. Where people were frustrated after two months, I was enjoying the solitude I had never gifted myself. I was so happy, so peaceful. I was finally myself.

Sadly enough, the lockdown had to end. Everybody went back to earn their living. Being a student back then, my upcoming routine was left undecided, an issue to be dealt with later. I didn't mind. But the day my parents went to work, lunch became a lonely affair. I missed them. That day, I wanted to call my mom up to tell her how delicious everything tasted, when she cooked for us. I wanted to fight with dad over the mouth-watering curry. I missed the bustling in the kitchen when everyone wanted to put in their effort and help in laying the table. Where once for years, no two people in the house had eaten their meals at the same time, let alone together, for those four months, nobody had eaten lunch alone.

Though I can't speak for everyone, for me the lockdown was the best thing that had happened at that time. It was the most needed, desired, and happy time of my life. The pandemic took a lot of lives, but it gave a new soul to our listless ones. Not only had I learnt the importance of taking a pause, spending time with family, and not getting carried away in a world full of mindless racing, but also of cherishing those little moments of camaraderie with friends, with kith and kin, which in the usual hustle-bustle of life had taken a backseat till then.

I often used to procrastinate making plans to meet the ones I once had so much in common with, namely, my friends; only because I was too lazy to socialise. This quarantine taught me a useful lesson—to treasure one's friends and relations and find time for them, come what may. Never again will I let go of a chance to meet someone under the excuse of 'I can meet them some other day.' Not having a phone just made it all better. Back then, I didn't know how I was going to survive without it. Now, I know how I did—happily.

Too Broken to Mend

@Anjali Dalal

Souls meet
Hold hands, mine in yours
On the astral plane, heartbeats amiss
Perfumes enmesh, make unfound bliss
Entwine.

We peep
See thoughts, read feelings
Three dimensional traps, captive in fief
Dungeons of sorrow, buried grief
Escape.

We caress
Tears and tarnish, emotional gashes
Ridicule of the inside, not seen outside
Lines within boundaries, servitude
Embrace.

We listen
All heard, unbridled desires
So many sounds—words spoken, unspoken
Muffled sighs, creaking hearts split open
Embolden.

Together mend
Click! That's the right fit, quivering peace, minds repair
That's the first light of sunlight, no more despair
Emend.

My Learnings from the Pandemic

@Aditi Lahiry

It all began in March 2020. Joy's teacher from PP2 class called me up,

'Hello Ma'am, Joy seems to have a little cold. We can't keep him in school, he might be having symptoms of Covid 19. Please come down as soon as possible and take him home.'

I clearly remember the date to be 13th of March. Amit had gone to Kolkata, to attend my father-in-law's cataract operation. My parents had arrived by the 15th night for Joy's sixth birthday celebrations on the 17th of March. It would be the first time that Amit would not be in the city during our only son's birthday.

We celebrated Joy's birthday at home with a few children attending the party. As days passed, things started turning out to be a little weird.

On March 22nd—a Sunday, a one-day lockdown was declared. By the 24th, almost a month-long lockdown was declared. None of the maids or cooks could enter inside the complex or any houses. Our driver, Kamal was also stopped from entering inside the complex. None of the delivery boys of Amazon or Flipkart could deliver the ordered goods at our doorsteps. The orders were delivered at the community gate of our apartment complex in Hyderabad, and we could collect them once during the day after completely sanitising them.

As I am an English and French Language trainer, I used to take classes from my home. Around ten to twelve children and adults used to come to my residence to attend the classes, but the lockdown changed the course of events completely. Day after day, we were confined indoors sans any domestic help. Many of my students requested me to continue the classes online.

After Amit returned from Kolkata on the twenty fourth, I asked him to download the Zoom app for me, through which I could connect with my students and continue with their classes.

The first month turned out to be a bit challenging, for we were introduced to the concept of work from home, and we continued doing the regular chores of home all by ourselves. Initially, walking around the complex was also confined, so we began to watch movies or play indoor games like Ludo or chess to keep the mind diverted from the disturbing news of the rising number of cases of people around us testing positive.

Much before the first month ended, announcement was made for the second month of quarantine. Amit's business based on marketing was also suffering due to this work-from-home scenario. Yet we were hoping for better days.

Meanwhile Joy my son kept himself occupied by mixing paints, colours, lotions, and creams to create something unique.

One day he ran up to me and declared,

'Mumma, see I have made the magic potion to cure Covid 19. This is the vaccine for Covid. If you just put two drops of it with a spoon, Covid-19 will vanish forever. Please use this.'

I wanted to believe Joy 's words and wished from the bottom of my heart that this mission of our scientists and doctors would be successful and this deadly pandemic, which had made us habituated to the 'new-normal' would forever end for all of us.

That Summer life changed for many of us. Wearing masks and stepping out, sanitising ourselves, maintaining social distancing, changing our clothes as soon as we returned from outside became a part of day-to-day routine. Meeting friends virtually, attending my son's first graduation too virtually, not having a summer vacation were all that we experienced within a span of the couple of months. The fear of the pandemic was increasing day by day.

Life had to go on, whether smooth or rough. We all stood strong saying this too shall pass. The maids were finally allowed to enter our complex once in a day. By June, Hriijoy's school reopened virtually. He began to attend his online classes for the first time ever. He was in his first grade. It was a new school. There was so much to learn and adjust. I used to sit with him to help him get with his classes. Then, as soon as his classes got over, my classes would begin.

My parents, who were supposed to return to Kolkata in April were struck in Hyderabad with us. In fact, it's they who gave us enough strength to survive through this most challenging period, the so-called Phase-1 of the pandemic before they could leave for Kolkata in July.

I began to meet my school friends virtually. Soon, I was introduced to a story telling group called *Maya-Katha* (mysterious story) and made some awesome friends. I started telling stories, recording them, and uploaded them on YouTube and *Maya-Katha* on the social media channel. Getting associated with Meera V. Barath and her venture *Maya-Katha* was the best thing that could have happened to me during the pandemic time. I was soon taking baby steps in the social media writing sites, 'Let's Make Stories Dino', 'The Pink Comrade', 'The Story Scrapers', 'My Words A Renaissance', 'Poetry Planet', 'Tunisian Asian Poetry', 'Chrysanthemum Chronicles', 'Artoons Inn poetry Planet', 'Beyond the Box' and 'Penmancy' became the virtual platforms, for which I began to write and contribute regularly. I made many friends, who are equally talented and creative while penning their thoughts on these platforms.

I was in awe to find that most of them kept themselves engaged by writing about one creative topic after another using their unique style and patience. Along with my regular chores, I spent a good amount of time on these virtual platforms and began to participate. They gave me a new opening and abundant opportunities. Before the year end my works written in the form of poems, stories and articles began to be published in various anthologies.

The beginning of 2021 gave me a new zeal to work. On 26th January 2021, I met up with most of my school friends and we enjoyed thoroughly after a long, long time. We sang and danced to the tunes of old Hindi movie songs. It was indeed a fun-filled day. However, these memories had to take a backstage as the pandemic appeared in a new avatar choking and leaving people breathless.

Soon cases began to rise, almost every family began to have at least one member who had tested positive. In April even my husband Amit tested positive. His ninety-year-old aunt had tested positive a week ago. Her oxygen levels kept falling drastically, so she was shifted to the hospital in the first week of April of that year. She battled against the disease and finally expired on the eleventh of April. The entire house lived in a realm of fear. Another of Amit's aunts who lived in Ranchi, tested positive too. The whole family including her son, daughter-in-law tested positive too, including her grandson who was pursuing his IIT course, though online since the last two years. This was the time, I wrote an article for an anthology titled, "The Impish Lass Requiem" for the Impish Lass Publishing House.

That summer vacation was equally disturbing. We shifted to a new apartment in January. Joy found a new friend for himself. He was a five-year-old boy named Niranjan, our next-door neighbour's son. He and Joy spent the whole summer vacation in the each other's company. It was only during Joy's seventh birthday that we managed to go for a trip to Chirala beach for three days. We enjoyed the trip thoroughly.

The next academic session too continued full swing with the online classes. We started with our first and second doses of vaccinations. Finally, in October, we were able to visit Kolkata after two years. We stayed there for two months. Hriijoy continued with his online classes from there.

My sister and brother-in-law joined us in November. They had been married only in November 2019 and had relocated to Brno in Czech Republic just weeks before the pandemic. They too had faced phases of lockdown, where even the borders were closed.

The last two years taught me to embrace every moment of life as it comes. It has taught me to be open to face any kind of challenge that life throws at you. I have become more adaptive, I have learnt to explore those hidden talents in me, my son Joy and all the children who are associated with me.

This pandemic has made us all emerge together and stay together as a close-knit family, and we learnt to help each other grow. Seen such wonderful examples of humanity. I feel extremely thankful to all my friends who have stood by my side during these challenging days. They have helped me grow. Best wishes to each of them. May they scale new heights and voice their opinion during difficult times. For I always believe in two things.

1. Everything happens for a very good reason.

2. Tough times don't last but tough people do.

Staying Under the Bell
Due to the Smog?

Covid Analogies from Mahabharata

@Gaurav Bhatia

Many of us might be revisiting our old comic stashes in these unprecedented Quarantine/ WFH times. I am no exception and while I sorted out my stuff consequent to my superannuation, I came across an old "Chandamama"—a magazine that was a staple for all school going kids—me and my elder sister (Vandana), being no different. As I flipped through the pages of the magazine, I came across this anecdote from the "18-day Kurukshetra Battle of Mahabharata". The hidden lesson which I found lurking in this old mythological story—surprised and profoundly affected me. I hope it will force you to rethink your response to the rapidly changing (worsening) COVID situation and the inevitable "Quarantine Days" that all of us were subjected to in the past.

Krishna, Arjuna & The Sparrow—An Invigorating Anecdote from Kurukshetra

The battlefield of Kurukshetra was being prepared to facilitate the movement of mammoth armies with large cavalries. They used elephants to uproot trees and clear the ground. On one such tree lived a sparrow, a mother of four young ones. As the tree was being knocked down, her nest landed on the ground along with her offspring—too young to fly—miraculously unharmed.

The vulnerable and frightened sparrow looked around for help. Just then she saw Krishna scanning the field with Arjuna. They were there to physically examine the battleground and devise a winning strategy before the onset of the war.

She flapped her tiny wings with all her might to reach Krishna's chariot.

'Please save my children, O Krishna,' the sparrow pleaded. 'They will be crushed tomorrow when this battle starts.'

'I hear you,' said He, the omniscient one, 'but I can't interfere with the law of nature.'

'All I know is that you are my saviour, O Lord. I rest my children's fate in your hands. You can kill them, or you can save them, it's up to you now.'

'The wheel of time moves indiscriminately,' Krishna spoke like an ordinary man implying that there wasn't anything he could do about it.

'I don't know your philosophy,' the sparrow said with faith and reverence. 'You are the wheel of time. That's all I know. I surrender to thee.'

'Stock food for three weeks in your nest then.'

Unaware of the ongoing conversation, Arjuna was trying to shoo away the sparrow when Krishna smiled at the bird. She fluttered her wings a few minutes in obeisance and flew back to her nest.

Two days later, just before the boom of conchs announced the commencement of the battle, Krishna asked Arjuna for his bow and arrow. Arjuna was startled because Krishna vowed to not lift any weapon in the war. Besides, Arjuna believed that he was the best archer out there.

'Order me, Lord,' he said with conviction, 'nothing impenetrable for my arrows.'

Quietly taking the bow from Arjuna, Krishna aimed at an elephant. But, instead of bringing the animal down, the arrow hit the bell around its neck and sparks flew.

Arjuna couldn't contain his chuckle seeing that Krishna missed an easy mark.

'Should I?' He offered.

Again, ignoring his reaction, Krishna gave him back the bow and said that no further action was necessary.

'But why did you shoot the elephant Keshav?' Arjun asked.

'Because this elephant had knocked down the tree sheltering that sparrow's nest.'

'Which sparrow?' Arjun exclaimed. 'Moreover, the elephant is unhurt and alive. Only the bell is gone!'

Dismissing Arjuna's questions, Krishna instructed him to blow his conch.

The war began, numerous lives were lost over the next eighteen days. The *Pandavas* won in the end. Once again, Krishna took Arjuna with him to navigate through the muddy field. Many corpses still lay there awaiting their funeral. The battleground was littered with severed limbs and heads, lifeless steeds, and elephants.

Krishna stopped at a certain spot and looked down thoughtfully at an elephant bell.

'Arjuna,' he said, 'will you lift this bell for me and put it aside?'

The instruction, though simple, made little sense to Arjuna. After all, in the vast field where plenty of other things needed clearing, why would Krishna ask him to move an insignificant piece of metal out of the way? He looked at him perplexed.

'Yes, this bell,' Krishna reiterated. 'It's the same bell that had come off the elephant's neck I had shot at.'

Arjuna bent down to lift the heavy bell without another question. As soon as he lifted it though, his world changed, forever.

One, two, three, four and five. Four young birds flew out one after another followed by a sparrow. The mother bird swirled in a circle around Krishna, circum-ambulating him in great joy. The bell cleaved eighteen days ago had protected the entire family.

'Forgive me O Krishna,' said Arjuna, 'Seeing you in the human body and behaving like ordinary mortals, I had forgotten who you are.'

The Hidden Lesson

The Forced Quarantine—Home/ Institutional, travel restrictions, work from home etc. (Mythological Bell) that we are being encouraged (some people may say forced) to adopt by the Government (Krishna)—must be taken at their face value and MUST NOT be resisted, questioned, or debated. All these are eventually aimed at our betterment and a COVID free future.

I am reminded of a quote by Robert Baden-Powell, which my school scoutmaster—Mr Ronald Parker would often repeat, and I feel it applies to all citizens of the world today:

One of the first duties of a Scout is obedience to authority. He must obey his orders in the first place and put his own amusement or desires in the second.

Mahabharata & Delhi Smog—The "Obscure" Connection!!

Before I start recounting the second anecdote, I will be failing if I do not take this opportunity to acknowledge five primaeval forces, which got me to reflect and write about this tale of enduring relevance.

- First is my fascination with Mahabharata as a multi-layered epic tale—which provides the reader with new and hitherto unseen perspectives, every time one revisits the tale. Despite having been written around 400 BC,

it remains relevant to the issues germane to our existence—as I will attempt to elucidate hereunder.

- The second was the comparative image of NOIDA shared by a dear classmate and long-time friend—Deepak Gidwani, a Senior Journalist from Lucknow. The image is replicated below with the caption that Deepak originally used to describe the image, 'The one on the left is from August 2020. And the one on the right is today in NOIDA.'

- The third is the play on the word *"Obscure"* which I was surprised to learn was an epithet for Heraclitus of Ephesus (535-475 BC), who was an Ancient Greek, pre-Socratic, Ionian philosopher and a native of the city of Ephesus, which was then part of the Persian Empire. His appreciation for wordplay and oracular expressions, as well as paradoxical elements in his philosophy, earned him the epithet *"The Obscure"* from antiquity. One such cryptic utterance by Heraclitus states, 'A hidden connection is stronger than an obvious one.'

- Fourth was the encouragement provided by Prof. Yash Daultani, Faculty Operations Management Group, Indian Institute of Management, Lucknow, who taught me the Operations Strategy elective in the Final Term.

- Last, but not least—my parents—Krishan & Reva Bhatia—who, despite their nascent IT skills, never fail to read everything I write—immaterial of the platform being utilised and always provide positive feedback.

Now let me come to the main intent of this piece:

Have a look at this graphic, which attempts to bring to fore the "obscure" connect that I alluded to earlier concerning Heraclitus between Mahabharata and how it remains relevant even today.

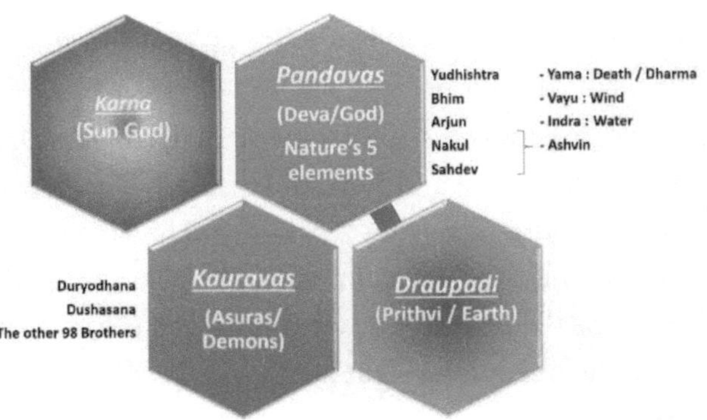

Allow me to elaborate on the slightly cryptic graphic:

- In the epic Mahabharata, Kurukshetra is the mother of all conflicts, the "Armageddon" of sorts, if you please.

- The ultimate fight between good (*Pandavas*—incarnations of *Devas*/Gods with their respective equivalence to the Natures five elements) & evil (*Kauravas*—incarnations of *Asuras*/Demons).

- *Draupadi*—the divine presence who was miraculously born as a fully-grown woman from the belly of the Earth's Fire.

- *Karna*—incarnate of the Sun God, identified by the Kavach and Kundal, which gave him his powers.

If you look closely at this treatise of the main characters and the storyline—the connection is so evident and beautiful to visualise—yet so "*Obscure*".

Sample these nuggets:

- The Pandavas (five elements of Nature) had to be united with Draupadi (Earth) to nourish it and Draupadi obviously could not under any circumstances be close to Karna (the Sun God incarnate).

- The disrobing of Draupadi by Dushasana on the explicit directions of Duryodhana (Asuras / Demons ⇔ Forces of Humanity) is akin to the pillaging/ unmindful stripping/ exploiting of the natural resources available on Earth. Quite reminiscent of the Humanities actions - we see all around us today, where the greed of the humans is destroying nature's abundant resources, faster than they can be replenished.

- The Pandavas loss to Kauravas in the game of dice—signifies to me the temporary defeat of Good by Evil.

- The 12 years of banishment from Hastinapur coupled along with the one year of incognito existence—of the Pandavas along with Draupadi, could be seen as the long spell of misery and misfortune (famine/drought/floods/other natural and anthropogenic disasters) which visit the Earth - with increasing frequency with each passing year, due to the intractable greed of humanity as a whole.

- The annihilation of humanity in the Kurukshetra battlefield—can be seen happening all around us, in this unprecedented COVID time, where nature seems to be saying what Theodore Roosevelt so prophetically stated a long time ago.

'To waste, to destroy our natural resources, to skin and exhaust the land instead of using it to increase its usefulness, will result in undermining in the days of our children the very prosperity which we ought by right to hand down to them amplified and developed.'

It would bode us well—for the future, if we were to remember what Phil Kingston stated.

'The more we take, the less there is for future generations.'

- Is COVID an indication of the Earth expressing its angst at our actions?

- Is the omnipresent smog/climate change indications (so evident in the Noida picture above) a warning sign for us to mend our ways and ensure that we preserve our Earth for future generations in line with the statement made by Theodore Roosevelt enumerated above—else we ought to be ready to face dire consequences.

Mutate: The Genesis

@Sandhita Agarwal

The monstrous pink hydra had its tentacles around her leg and the more she struggled to swim to the surface the more it pulled her back into the abyss where it lived. Her mind gave up first and soon her body followed, slowly as the pink tentacle dragged her into the watery depths of hell, blackness overcame her.

She woke up with a start. The same dream. The same sweat drenched mornings and the same expanse of a life that stretched out like a vast dark cavern in front of her.

She dreaded the trip back home. Meandering roads led home and her wandering mind was never able to keep up with the bends in the road. Mark had promised to take her home but lately their habitual fights had taken on a metallic quality, a certain aftertaste, like food kept open in the fridge for too long. He had slept at his workplace last night and she felt guilty for enjoying his absence.

As the sun opened shop for the day, she climbed into her black Camry and started the arduous journey home. Home, she still called that place home. But she was a nomad now, a Bedouin of the world. She was twenty-eight and she still had not found home. The apartment was Mark's. The place she was driving to belonged to her parents. Where was her home?

She slowly depressed the gas pedal as she pushed the habitants of her mind to the back. Her body began tensing up. She chanted the mantra over and over under her breath. I can do this. I can do this.

The traffic was bad as usual in the city. Every near-miss bumper dash made her head hurt and her jaw clench more. Once she was out on the highway, she began to relax a little. The billboards passed by, and she struggled to keep her mind focused on the road. But memories of him began to eagerly flood this vacuum of her head, like scores of ants hoarding over a dead moth.

'It's a fucking pop-up restaurant!' he said. The moment she had heard the word pop-up she had left the piece of code she was working on and rushed to her room. Ten minutes later, she was ready in blue jeans and a tee. They had excitedly gotten into his car and drove to the trendy eating-place. She loved him a lot, but she loved food more. She laughed excitedly at the thought. Whenever she ate something that satiated her, she would tell him how much she loved him, and he would laugh and tease her. It's just that food made her feel happy about being alive, good food was like a drug. He took her hand in his while driving. This was their thing. They always did that. It was their ritual. A way of communicating through the silence of their relationship. He didn't speak much. He wasn't expressive. She was the one who regaled him with her stories. Or so she thought.

She was almost 'home'. She was swallowing a large pill of happiness mixed with trepidation and guilt. She didn't know why she felt dread every time she came home. She knew but she chose to pretend to not know. Because knowing is what cements a thought or a feeling. And she didn't want to give air to this monster of an idea that was always lurking at the bottom of her being.

She rang the bell on the porch. Soon the door opened, and the happy visage of her mother was visible through the brown doorway. She hugged the frail woman and kissed on her leathery wrinkled cheek.

Her mother looked healthier and happier. That made the guilt lessen a bit. Then she saw her dad. The once strapping tall man was now reduced to a framework of bones that struggled to keep the powerful man supported. The thin bones worked hard to support the weight of his personality. He was sometimes like a black hole, powerful and sucking in all light. She had often seen strange lacunas in her mother, areas completely empty and void. Pat could already feel parts of herself ebbing away in the night travelling over miles to reach her father.

Her father hugged her, and she relaxed a bit. They sat down to a decadent feast. Her mother and Linda - the help, had prepared a feast in her honour. All her favourite things, from steak and mash to spaghetti. She stuffed herself till she couldn't breathe. She felt happy for that moment and only happy, not the amalgamate of feelings she usually was.

She went to her room upstairs. The room where she had spent twenty years of her life. The room that was hers and still felt foreign, a no man's land between her present and her past. The window looked out into the main street, where rows of houses sat on either side of the road, dark, empty, and dead.

She often dreamt of canine creatures—lions, tigers, leopards, and their likes attacking her. These were dreams full of running, hiding, and being stalked by these creatures. She sometimes had fun in these dreams, the adrenaline pumping through her veins. But most days she woke up with a start in the middle of the night, frightened. And as her conscious mind woke up from its slumber, her racing heart would soften its pace, and she would sink back into reality. These days it was the hydra-dream that was interjecting between lucid dreams of finding treasures and becoming a social media star.

The house was a red brick structure, newly built. But she often heard ancient whispers in the house. Whispers that criticised her. One night when she was fifteen, she had got out of bed to find the source of these nocturnal murmurs. She followed the sounds to her parents' bedroom. She slowly opened the door to peer inside. The sounds seemed to be coming from her parents. Were they talking about her in the night? She shone her flashlight at the bed, her parents were fast asleep and yet she could hear the unholy rumblings. The blood left her face as her mind grappled with the impossibility of what she was seeing. The sounds suddenly increased in intensity. She wanted to scream and wake her parents up. But her instincts told her it was pointless. She had never been a brave child, but this moment felt like the articulation of what was and what would be. She moved towards the bed and crouched down. She lifted the bedsheets up from over the space where monsters lived in movies and children's stories. And there she saw what she knew she would see. And would carry with her for the rest of her life.

She woke up at 2 a.m. to the familiar whispers. Her heart sank. She had hoped that things had changed, that time had erased those shadows in the house. This time the whispers portended something new. The same echoes inferring a different song this time. It wasn't their usual notes of chides and jibes. There was a new note here, an underlying threat to the whole chanson. She heard them whisper all night, but she didn't get up to investigate. There was nothing more to see and nothing more to understand.

The news next day frightened her. A new kind of virus had been found in China. She had been frightened the first time she had heard of Zika virus and Nipah virus. She loved watching zombie movies because the thrill of the impossibility of those stories made her feel alive. This new virus scared her more than any other had done.

Back in Mark's apartment, she found the familiar walls unwelcoming, she felt as if she had entered a hostile parallel universe. They sat across from each other enjoying the meal that Mark had made. The silence was thick this time. She wondered why; had she done something to offend him? 'The burrito tastes amazing,' she said. 'Ya,' Mark replied. She could feel the familiar guilt rising. Why had she let him cook? She could have brought something from home. He had insisted and wanted to surprise her. But then, what had changed in the two hours between her call and her return? The anxiety was like a knot in her throat. She felt foolish for even feeling anxious. 'Are you okay?' she anxiously enquired. 'Ya, why?' Mark replied tersely. 'You're not saying anything.' She coaxed him on. 'What am I supposed to say?' and with that she stopped probing him. After dinner she went for a walk to escape the stifling atmosphere of the apartment. Where was home? She asked herself again. When she returned, Mark was glued to his PS4. She went into the bedroom, popped her usual Xanax, and fell asleep.

She endured Mark's silent treatment for days, not knowing what her fault was. He refused to talk and would just sulk. She tried making him his favourite dishes, tried pleasing him in bed but she could not placate him. A mute and deaf statue of a great martyr. Then out of the blue things were normal again.

Like a gigantic eight-legged spider creature Covid was scuttling towards her country. It was all over the news. It was like a real-life *Contagion* movie. Her dad didn't believe it would reach their sleepy town. It was a disease of the East. She was paranoid. Like any good geek she stocked up on MRE meals, hand sanitisers and masks. Mark called her a fool.

Then it hit her country. The first case. Then the first death. She made sure her parents had stocked up on frozen and dried food and the necessities. She knew she shouldn't encourage stock piling, but she was scared for her parents. The disease apparently affected the elderly and the immunocompromised group more severely. Her mother was a cancer survivor, and her dad was a living potpourri of diseases like diabetes, asthma, heart disease, and what not. She was too scared to watch the news. Her heart was always heavy with guilt and concern for her parents. When she tried to get some comfort from Mark, he was as usual unavailable, brushing her concerns off with just a 'everything will be fine'. Everybody at work was on edge. Her performance at work suffered greatly because she was always anxious. Then the lock down happened. She was relieved in a way. Her faith in the government had been wavering and this was a welcome move. This thing would end. They would all be fine. She wanted to believe that. She decided to visit her parents before the lockdown was put in place. Mark was completely against it, but she couldn't take all the worrying any longer. She needed to be there for a while at least. She left her sulking boyfriend and made the journey home. She had taken the day off from work and would be doing work from home till the lockdown ended.

The roads seemed lonelier than ever. Like the calm before a storm. The world was now an alien place, a place where the impossible didn't exist anymore. The impossible existed only inside of her.

Her parents seemed happy to see her, she thought with relief. They seemed oddly cheerful in light of the status quo of the world. Maybe they were aliens who flourished in adversity while normal life made them sad shells of their usual selves. Or maybe they were just happy to see her and not feel alone anymore.

To be continued…

Mutate: The Ossification

@Sandhita Agarwal

Covid got worse and worse. Thousands of deaths every day. As Covid sunk its teeth into her little country, fear sunk its teeth into hers. She was constantly assailed by worries of her parents dying, that the microscopic murderer would find its way into their homes. Days were spent laying rigid protocols in place. Their backyard had become a military post, a processing plant where things were first decontaminated before being introduced into the home. Social interactions with neighbours were nulled. Trips outside were avoided. Their lives were confined to the four walls of their house. She tried to forget everything that relaxed her, trips to restaurants, travel to hill stations and also things which stressed her like Covid and Mark. Mark kept insisting on her returning, but she couldn't. She couldn't leave her parents alone. She knew it was her burden to bear but she wished he would understand. His parents had lots of relatives and neighbours who took care of them. But her parents were loners, social outcasts who had shunned the warmth of society early on because they considered the common people to be plebians. She was always torn between her duties, love for her parents and Mark. The conversations with Mark were scathing. They tore her from the inside. She couldn't believe the things he said sometimes. Did he really have such vile thoughts about her? He always apologised at the end though.

The lockdown never lifted, and a year passed. There was no visible end to the pandemic. It was an interminable chapter in their lives. A never-ending story of deaths, fear, uncertainty, and hopelessness. There were stories of businesses closing, rampant unemployment, depression, and divorces. On the upside the lockdown had given people time to procreate.

She had blocked Mark on all platforms and had stopped replying to his emails, emails swinging between promises of eternal love and scathing jibes. One day when she was cooking, she cut her finger. She didn't feel the pain much but what shocked her was the brownish-grey metallic skin under her normal skin. She peeled off a part of the first layer of epidermis to find another layer underneath, a leather-metallic grey skin, which was hard like bark to the touch. Her hypochondria immediately kicked in. She left her cooking and went online to scour texts for similar conditions. But found nothing. She didn't want to panic her parents so hid it from them. But she was afraid that she had some terminal condition. Or maybe she had caught a new mutation of covid. She isolated herself for a week in her room on the pretext of working on a big project. But she developed no other symptoms. Her anxiety had hit the roof. She had visible twitches and she couldn't control the twitching of her hands anymore. She finally decided to show the second skin to her parents. The wound had almost healed. She peeled off a tiny part but was astonished to see flesh underneath. She was now convinced she was either losing her mind or had some weird disease.

This was the first symptom in a series of symptoms that would affect her.

Her dad was on the phone with her sister who lived abroad. And her sister made a joke. And even though she knew it was funny and she felt the laughter stuck somewhere at the back of her throat, but she just couldn't laugh. The whole act of laughing suddenly felt foreign to her, as if laughter was a lesson learnt way back in school, familiar and unfamiliar at the same time. She tried watching old tv shows that used to have her in splits. Nothing. She was an alone, unlaughable woman now with a second disappearing leather-metal skin.

She had battled with depression and anxiety for the majority of her life, but this was different. She felt different. Not a good or bad different, simply different. Covid different maybe?

Covid was mutating quickly, creating new RNAs and spikes in itself, becoming more contagious and virulent. And Covid was also mutating people. Changing them in unpredictable ways. It wasn't only the residual depression, anxiety, or the myocardial after-effects of the Covid recovered, it was changing never-caught-Covid people into something different. Something that they themselves couldn't recognise for better or for worse. Maybe people keep mutating all their life or maybe they mutate according to the occasion.

She remembered the first time Mark had mutated. It was a few days after she had moved in with him. They were eating ice-cream together. She didn't really have a sweet tooth, but she loved him feeding her. And he loved ice-creams. He had gone to get more ice-cream from the fridge and had left his phone behind. She picked up his phone. Back then they had no phone lock patterns and let each other peruse their phones at will. She opened his gallery to look at the pictures that he had taken of her a few hours ago at the dinner with his friends. She found a folder named sweets. In that she found scores of pictures of scantily clad ultra-fit women with giant derrieres. She was a bit shocked.

Maybe she had believed that she was the only person he would ever be interested in. She didn't know what to believe then. She checked the dates on the pics and the last one was yesterday. It creeped her out. She felt as if she didn't even know him. She knew about his obsession with her butt. But was he really one of those creeps who ogled women?

As soon as she thought about this, she remembered the first time she had met him. It was right after her breakup with Daniel. She had gone with a company that arranged treks. She had met Mark on that trek. He was not an attractive person. But he was funny. And they had become good friends on the trek. But one thing that had always put her off even on the trek was his habit of ogling pretty women. Even after they started hanging out together, she would catch him ogling in a very lecherous way. This was one of the reasons why he hadn't been on her boyfriend material list. But he always made her laugh. They used to have long conversations about women empowerment and the nature of human beings. And one day he proposed. She wasn't ready for it. She was caught off guard. And he was showering so much attention on her. And now looking back that is what she had needed, attention and validation. It all came back to her. She had caught him multiple times and ticked him off. And they had had huge fights about it. And she hadn't caught him doing it again. To be honest, him looking at other women triggered her own insecurities about her looks and her worth. And maybe all men looked at other women. But after they had gotten together, she couldn't even look at another man and here he was, with vulgar images of women. Was he jerking off to these women in the bathroom? He saw her with the phone and the pics. She started teasing him about it and he got angry quickly. He told her to mind her own business. She was shocked at his rebuttal. She reminded him that he was her boyfriend, and this was her business. And it further horrified her when he said he didn't want to be her boyfriend anymore and regretted her moving in. And that was when he mutated.

His face became livid contorting into a grotesque reflection of his visage. It scared her. And with that 'gargoylean' mouth, he told her that he was going to slap her if she didn't shut up. And she did shut up after that. She was made to listen to a lengthy soliloquy about how it was her fault. How it was just a group of guys who sent such pictures and didn't mean anything. And she believed him. She apologised for overreacting. She was scared of losing him. This was the first of many such incidences. Many such mutations. Mutations of his self, of her and of their relationship.

Mark had apologised and promised to change, to never get angry that way, to never use the things she had told him in confidence as ammunition during their fights, to never talk of throwing her out every time they fought, to never threaten to slap her or actually slap her if she didn't shut up, to never tell her that she was a loser, to never tell her that she was fat and that women with babies had lost weight, to never make her feel worthless or unwanted. She had been weak without him. It felt good to have him back.

Her parents were undergoing certain mutations too. They had somehow resigned themselves to this life, to this life of hiding out. They had always been social outcasts, but they seemed cheerful in their little dominion. Their mutations were affecting her and hers, them. She was like them, slowing down. Everything around her seemed to be slowing down. Days, nights, people, news, food, and time. Her work and Mark kept her barely alive. They were her tethers to the world.

She knew that the mutation was twisting into macabre forms inside her, when she realised the horror movies that used to give her so much pleasure made no sense now. The adrenaline that used to pump through her veins when she used to play horror video games was replaced by a stream of tepid saline water. She realised the intensity of her transformation when she calmly told Mark to fuck-off and blocked him. The shackles of guilt and shame that had forever imprisoned her in her own mind were gone. Poof. Like Magic. And that was life for you.

Her mutagenesis was complete the day she lost words. Words which had been her friends since childhood, words which had hurt her, and also comforted her, words which had been her haven, had abandoned her. This completed her metamorphosis into someone she didn't recognise. But she didn't question the new her. Her parents noticed her new self, quieter, graver yet emitting a new kind of strength. She scared them now.

To be continued…

Mutate: The Redemption

@Sandhita Agarwal

Days blended into nights, and it was day again. Everywhere around her people had started going back to their normal lives. Her friends who were not her friends invited her to restaurants, to soirees, to movies, to treks, to the gym. She wanted to go, she badly wanted to feel normal again, to feel something again. She could wear a N95 mask and meet her friends who were not her friends in the park. But she didn't want to. She realised she couldn't take the risk with her parents there. After watching and reading and hearing about people die from Covid, she had had enough. She would wait. She would wait for this monster to go away—she would wait for the sun to rise again, and she would wait to feel like herself again. Or maybe the transformation was permanent. Was it a good thing?

She spent her time working and reading and watching Netflix. Netflix had become this black hole that sucked everything in, all the sadness, the hopelessness, the joy, the excitement, the hunger, the blasé. It was a bottomless pit of a person who ate whatever she fed him.

Mark's emails had finally ceased. Mark was a guy from a past life. A man without a face, a man with just her stolen words and her stolen feelings. She was thankful that he had stopped because his emails made her remember things she didn't want to.

They were celebrating the new year together at a party. She was going to move in the following week, and they were happy and in love as couples are. They were dancing, there was music, there was laughter, and then there was anger. 'You slapped me,' Mark had said. 'No, what. I didn't,' she had shouted over the music. He had started walking away leaving her alone on the floor. What had just happened, she thought? She was drunk but not so much that she forgot anything. She followed him out of the hotel. He was walking ahead. She ran to him and asked him what his problem was. He grabbed at her throat and told her that he was hungry, and he had kept on insisting that they go have food and she was too busy enjoying herself to notice his needs. He started choking her. She started crying and he at once, let her go. She ran back into the hotel and locked herself in the bathroom. She was scared. She had never expected this from him. He soon came to the bathroom door and started weeping, 'You slapped me that's why I did what I did. You did it in front of friends. And I was hungry. I couldn't think properly.'

Why? Why did she acquiesce to his imploring? Why did she believe him when he said she deserved what she got? Why did she move in with him? Why did she tolerate years of mistreatment? Why did she let him steal a piece of her broken self? Why hadn't she loved herself the way she loved herself now?

She had finally become invisible. People at work could see her, her parents could see her and her friends too. But she couldn't see herself. Her mirror was an empty blankness. She liked that. She liked feeling invisible yet omnipotent because being invisible meant that nothing could hurt you. How would it if the hurt couldn't see you?

They were wave surfing now, riding out the first wave, then the second, the third and the fourth. She was good at it. Good at balancing her psyche on the thin board of reality. Sometimes she would lie awake at night listening to the deaths of the people in the world. The newspapers were full of optimism. About elections, and government changes, hunting down businesspeople who stole from the banks, about billionaire businessmen going into orbits around the Earth, and labelling themselves the first men into space. There were also floods, cyclones, earthquakes, collapsing buildings that swallowed the common folks like giant whales, while the rich were left untouched. But Covid had been an impartial murderer. It had only one MO (modus operandi) kill, kill, kill. It spread its many arms long and wide and didn't spare the elite either. The veteran actor, the young upcoming star, and the young billionaire businessman were all hunted down by Covid and killed. She just sat in her swivelling chair and watched. The dance of the world. The passing of the world.

Then again, the calm before the next wave. Her friends had started dating and made new loves. But she was still waiting for her time. Her friends who were definitely not her friends anymore called her out to parties and soirees and restaurants and movies and the gym. And she couldn't. But this time it was different. She was waiting and waiting. There were news reports of Covid dying out, but she didn't believe them. How could Covid be mutating and dying out? It was a man-made virus, a super virus, it wouldn't die out till the world chose to eradicate it or lessen its impact. But the newspapers were adamant. She stared at the news reports, but they didn't change. She asked her cheerful-sad-angry dad about it. And he regurgitated what the newspaper had said. She was confused and she didn't like being confused. She would wait.

Her government soon ordered that people no longer needed to wear masks. But still she waited. Her company asked the employees to re-join work, but she took a long sick leave and waited. Her parents told her to go out, they were going and meeting friends who were not their friends. They were meeting people they hadn't been friends with. They were happy-sad-angry. But she still waited. Then her dad came to her room and slapped her. She felt something after a long time. It made her smile. He called her a psycho and left the room. She had finally felt something, but it wasn't pain.

There was the beach, there was the sun, and they were there. They were lying on the chaise lounges on the beach and drinking. That's what they did since they arrived on the island. Eat, drink and sleep. She wanted to go dancing but she knew after the new year fiasco the word dancing made him angry. She was starting to feel slightly sick. He wanted to go into the water. She told him to carry on and she returned to the room.

Back at the room, her nausea overtook her, and she retched into the toilet bowl. What had she eaten? She had been eating and drinking and not even getting any exercise. Because all he wanted to do was lie on the beach and chill. She got into the bed and was asleep. She heard him come in the room. 'Are we even going to go out again today?' he pouted. 'Maybe in the night. I just threw up.' she replied. 'You always eat too much.' He left the room. She was still on the bed when he returned in the evening. As soon as he saw her, he started screaming at her. 'You always ruin everything. You ruined this holiday too. Why did you have to eat so much?' She didn't have the strength to reply. 'Look at me when I am talking to you,' he had said. He pulled her up and punched her in the stomach. 'Now maybe you'll feel better.' The shock of the punch scared her more than the pain did. He left the room quickly.

That was the day she had decided to leave him. She cried and cried but she didn't have anyone to tell what had happened. She knew her parents would ask her to leave him. But she was scared of living life alone again. When she heard the doorknob turn, she was scared. But he was smiling. A glass of lemon juice and some pills were all that had taken to win her back. He hadn't even apologised. His only excuse was that she had made him mad. Because she always overreacted to everything.

Her dad's slap was like the kiss of breath for her. There was a hissing coming from herself, like vacuum being filled with something, something not air, herself. She was filling herself with herself again. She waited for the hissing to complete and when it was over, she rummaged around the insides of her being. It felt new yet familiar. There were new structures where old had been but for the most part it was the same.

She stepped out into the street. It felt familiar. But she felt scared. She took baby steps to the nearest store. She was the only one in a mask. People looked weirdly at her. So now I am the weirdo in a mask?

She slowly took off her mask. She felt naked as if she had exposed herself in public. But the breeze felt good on her lips, and she smiled.

She was finally going on the trek that she had planned for months. It was more difficult than her last trek, but she had been training for it well. The trekking company was the same. It felt like closure. The others were waiting for her at the airport. She saw them and smiled. It was an all-female only group. This trek was going to be the best trek ever.

Love Regained

@Hishita Lakhani

24th March 2020

Engrossed in her novel with a cup of strong black coffee, some romantic Hindi songs playing in the background, Naina missed Kabir's continuous calls on her mobile. Suddenly her ten-year-old daughter barged into her room with the landline in her hand, 'Yes papa, mama is right here with her favourite music, coffee and books.' Naina pulled the phone from Kiara's hand. 'Hello? You were calling? What's so urgent Kabir?' 'Why were you calling continuously?' Kabir was angry and furious, but he controlled himself. 'Put on the TV and watch the news, Naina. PM Modi has just announced a 21-day nation lockdown,' he said.

'A lockdown?' She blurted into the phone. 'Today? Why? What happened?'

'No time to waste Naina, I am running to the supermarket, quickly send me a list of all the important grocery and home essentials we will need for the next few weeks,' Kabir said.

Naina's hands trembled. She had never heard of or witnessed a lockdown before. But without wasting much time she jotted a long list of things on her phone and sent it to Kabir on WhatsApp (of course with a lot of interruption and pings from different school groups and kitty groups of panicked ladies and moms).

She quickly put on the TV and heard the speech where the Prime Minister was addressing the nation and advising all the citizens to abide to the rules from 12 o'clock midnight today and not to step out unless very urgent. The covid cases were increasing at an alarming rate and all the hospitals were getting full. The situation was out of control and the only way to curb it was a lockdown. The thought of this scared her. She had always been a very fearful girl, a bit timid too and would start stressing over smallest of issues.

Her phone pinged again. It was an email from Kiara's school stating that they would remain closed until further notice. She tried to calm herself, muttering to herself that everything would be okay soon, but mere the thought of Kiara and Kabir home 24/7 horrified her and started her palpitations.

Kabir and she were married for almost twelve years now. He had been an attentive, caring and very warm and loving husband for the first few years. Everything was beautiful and blissful. But over the past few years, the picture had gradually changed. Kabir had got more and more engrossed with work, and he hardly had any time for her and Kiara. His office commitments, after work meetings and parties with colleagues started straining their marriage. Naina felt left-out and hurt as she was always busy with household chores and taking care of Kiara's needs. Slowly the rift widened, and they drifted apart. She tried to make amends but was stonewalled by his attitude. Whenever she suggested something, he would give a pretext of work commitments. Frustrated, she started spending more time on social media.

After marriage, she had drifted apart from her friends, but now she touched base with them again. Time was spent happily chatting, what with same old forwards, some light-hearted banter, and jokes. She didn't even realise when she and Rishab (her first college crush) got so close that they started chatting and seeing each other on zoom calls every day. With Kabir being so busy and coming home late every day, she got attracted to Rishab and spoke to him for hours at a stretch. Rishab was giving her all the attention she was actually craving for, from Kabir. Rishab had really liked Naina in college, and she too had a crush on him. But because he wasn't settled then and her parents were very keen to get her married then, they both didn't pursue their relation further and she had got married to Kabir.

Naina quickly called Rishab, 'Hi, it's me, did you hear of the lockdown?'

'Yes dear, I am just rushing to pick up a few essentials. I will message you tonight on Instagram DM. Wait for me, Sweety.' She burst out crying. 'But Kabir will be home and around for next couple of weeks. How will we chat and do our private zoom calls, Rishab?'

'You don't stress, Naina; we will find a way. Don't panic, darling. I am with you,' said Rishab. Naina knew in her heart what she had with Rishab was definitely more than a friendship and maybe she was wrong, but she couldn't control her feelings for him.

Naina then called her parents to check if they were okay and advised them to be very careful and alert. Since the time the first covid case was detected in India, in first week of March, things had not been the same. This new virus which no one had ever heard of (where it came from?) had spread fast. Her phone suddenly rang. *'Bhabhi, kal se kaam par nahi aaunga* (Sister, I won't be coming to work from tomorrow), sab bandh hain (everything is closed).' It was her part time servant. She knew she was in a big soup now, realisation struck her—this is what exactly this lockdown meant. No servants, no cooks, no drivers, no help at all. She dreaded the thought that from the next day she would be doing all the household chores by herself.

Kabir got home and they unpacked all the essentials. They all had dinner in a quiet and grim atmosphere, each busy in their thoughts while watching the news in the background. He was so exhausted after a long day he fell asleep immediately after going to bed. Meanwhile Naina had a good one-hour chat with Rishab and that was actually the best part of her day.

March 25th 2020

Naina opened her eyes. it was 11.00 a.m. She didn't see Kabir on bed and went to check on him. 'Yes Madam, Good morning. I have been up since 8 a.m. What time did you sleep last night, you couldn't wake up this morning? Kiara was so hungry that I made her a cheese toast, and I had my black coffee. Really hungry now, can you quickly prepare some nice omelette for me?' This was exactly what she was dreading. Starting and ending her day with serving her husband and fulfilling all the duties of a dutiful wife and mother. She made a face, went to freshen up and began her day.

Kiara was happy with no school and was catching up on her favourite Bollywood movies while Kabir was engrossed in a long zoom call with his long-lost college buddies all over the world. He had no time to check on her or help her with any of the household chores. She got very angry with him but spent her time thinking she would end the day with her long chat with Rishab. But things didn't work in her favour. Since Kabir was home and on an enforced holiday, he wanted to binge watch. So, she had to stay awake with him watching some Netflix series. Scared of getting caught, she messaged Rishab saying they would chat the next day and she crashed in a few minutes of lights out.

✶✶✶✶

March 26th 2020

9.30 a.m.

'Naina. Please wake up. How much do you sleep? We are hungry. Cook us some delicious poha for breakfast,' announced Kabir. She snapped back at him. 'Why don't you cook it for yourself and make some for me too?' Kabir was astonished to hear her tone and left her alone. Naina freshened up and got back to the household chores. It was only second day of the lockdown, and she hated every bit of it. Meanwhile, her friends on WhatsApp groups were discussing how they were enjoying this time with their families. They were playing games, drinking wine, eating delicious food. How come? Here the picture was completely different. Were their husbands helping them with chores? Why wasn't Kabir doing the same? These questions played on her mind repeatedly. She was struggling to juggle all the responsibilities that suddenly fell on her shoulders, and she was having a hard time dealing with Kabir's indifference towards her and him having more expectations of her when he himself was always busy with work calls or leisure calls with his friends.

That night she cried herself to sleep. She had always loved Kabir a lot. What had changed that he no longer felt the same? Sometimes she wished I could actually press the rewind button and go back to the early years of their marriage. Those were the best years when he was so caring and affectionate, and he kept lingering around her. Will it ever be the same?

This routine went on for next few days, and Naina was so tired by the day's end, not to talk of boredom. She was missing her part time helpers and prayed for things to get back to pre-lockdown days. She was longing to go see her parents and spend time with them. She tried telling her mom about Kabir not helping out and how they were never on the same page, but her mom expectedly took his side saying that Kabir is a wonderful father and a loving husband, she should give her relation another chance and try to mend things rather than thinking of leaving him.

One morning she got up with a sore throat and had body pain too. Kabir panicked and rushed her to the doctor and did the necessary tests. The family doctor prescribed her some anti-biotics and medicines and could sense something was wrong between the couple. They were not only his patients but close friends too. He took Kabir aside to talk. He was shocked and was surprised to know Kabir was of no help to Naina and she was managing everything herself. He then explained to Kabir how the whole world was in this pandemic and trying to fight it and women were having a tough time and they needed their partner's support, running the house literally and figuratively.

He told Kabir to help Naina and reduce her burden. He should spend time with her, pamper her and care for her. 'She deserves it, Kabir. You are such a warm and loving couple. You both have been the best support system for each other over the years. Don't let anything or anyone ruin that please,' said Dr Akash. This small chat was an eye opener for Kabir, who resolved to be a better partner for Naina and a good father to Kiara.

She woke up the next morning with Kabir shaking her awake. She had tested negative. They breathed a sigh of relief. She couldn't imagine both Kabir and Kiara managing for 14 days without her. Kabir asked her to get some rest while he prepared breakfast for all of them. Naina was too weak to move anyways.

The next few days Kabir did most of the work at home. He made sure Naina was getting enough rest and he didn't mind keeping his office work pending. He helped her with the laundry, cooking, doing the dishes etc. The atmosphere at home was jovial. He was spending more time with Kiara too. Playing board games, puzzles, reading books, watching movies.

When Kabir would sleep at night and it was time for Rishab and Naina's chat, she would always make excuses and end it quickly. She realised that she was using Rishab all this time to vent out her issues with Kabir. She decided to take a step back and messaged him that she would call him once the lockdown was over.

For the first time in many years Kabir and Naina were actually spending quality time and rediscovering each other. They looked forward to their time alone when Kiara would go to bed, and they would snuggle up and watch some movies and chat about so many things. Naina secretly felt thankful for her illness and thanked Dr Akash for his timely intervention. It actually made their relation stronger and healthier. They both were coming out of their respective wells and were ready for each other. Their young love was now replaced with honesty and understanding and an openness to welcome new beginnings. Actually, nothing had changed but still something was different. They were eventually rekindling the long-lost love.

The lockdown went on for another month and slowly and gradually things started opening up. Kabir was working for a few hours in the day and dedicated all his free time to Naina and Kiara. He would take them once a week to her parents' place and they would all spend some lovely family time together.

June 10th 2020

The lockdown was finally over, and everyone breathed a sigh of relief. Of course, there were still so many covid cases and everyone was taking the necessary precautions but as they say, Life moves on—people were more aware and understood how to take care of themselves.

'I quite liked being locked down,' said Naina.

'Why do you say so?' asked Kabir.

'There was something missing Kabir, that spark, it got rekindled thanks to the lockdown.'

'Yes, I totally agree with you Naina. I will forever be grateful for the time I got with you and Kiara. I was beginning to be selfish. But thanks to the lockdown I actually realised my mistakes and am so happy I accepted them, and I am taking the effort to do the best I can. I can never think about losing you Naina. You are and will always be my true love. Forgive me for acting otherwise.'

Naina was feeling so content and full of gratitude in her heart. She was blessed with such a sensible and loving husband. She thanked God silently for directing her on the right path and ending things with Rishab before they got murkier. That was something she would take to her grave. Lockdown taught her many lessons but the most important one was, family is the most important thing in the world. She held Kabir's hand and drifted into a deep peaceful sleep.

Fourteen Days of Isolation

@Donna Nongkhlaw

If the menacing sound of COVID 19 was not entwined to my
period of isolation,
I would have happily embraced the two weeks of seclusion.
I would have jumped at the chance to rest my aching body
and stretch my tired bones,
It has been decades since I've been able to escape to
a fantasy land, flying,
Carried away by dreams that belonged to the sun.
I would have absconded happily from all the noise
That clogged and choked my deepest thoughts,
but today is a different story.

Spending my days in 'isolation' and waiting
Waiting for this disease to manifest its ugly form
Is not something I look forward to
But it does not know me. I have always been my own knight.
I willed every cell of my body to fight for me twice as much
To chase the little monsters that haunt me into deep abyss,
I devour the pages of a book.

Getting lost in its narrow streets overgrown by wild lilies
feeling every giggle and every sigh as if they were my own,
I drown myself into the incantation of musical waves
allowing every note to sink into my veins
like a magic potion healing me from within.
(And I feel fine).

They shouldn't know they have me cornered and alone,
I won't let them.
So, I decided to have a conversation with the Walls.
I didn't ask for permission
they too, never said a thing but absorbed every syllable I let out,
It was refreshing—a treat, rather.
For once, I talked without worry of lurking shadows,
I poured out my heart to them, all my dreams and aspirations.
All my thoughts that would otherwise never experience daylight
Unlike the uncovering of Qumran,
All my confessions
And they listened without a glimpse of judgement.

I have them fooled
The Couches in the living room, perched against the wall,
As if lying in wait for a prey to devour.
They looked at me as I turned to the Piano,
Who, in excitement, burst out in a shout.

We let out a laugh and engaged in sweet little banter,
The pictures on the wall
From garden parties of old and parasols,
All frozen in time, were keenly listening
hoping to experience life once again through my eyes.
(And I feel fine)

I looked out of my window, breathe in, breathe out
I could feel the air filling my lungs.
There, in the room, was a cupboard and a bed.
Oh, how cold they seemed, always covered in clothes,
The bed offered a smile, shrouding her grief.
Perhaps for the secrets she holds,
How long can she withstand her night-time fits?
'You're not alone.' I whispered
She wrapped me up in her blanketed arms,
I confessed my fears to her as she wiped my tears away.
Braced up, we swallow the pain of our momentary glitch,
Thence leaning back to our sanely self.

My favourite company is, however, the chattering pots and pans
Ever so generous to all that walks in,
Though for now they cater to me alone.

They labour all day to feed the cups and plates,
Without a doubt, the noisiest of the neighbours.
But I found comfort amidst their rambling,
Thus, dawning an epiphany, *I am but a social being.*
I needed my people, I yearned for their chatter,
It didn't take long for me to paint an image of their hugs
And reminisce their soft kisses.
The whistling kettle woke me up from my trance,
'She's a steamy little thing,' said Pots
while giving me food to strengthen my body,
But much more heals my soul.
(Yes, I feel fine, two days until absolution).

Lockdown Wedding

@Manobhi Maltare

Positive thinking is also a medicine that eliminates our negative thinking, due to which we see peace in the whole universe, and we can live a happy life. Hope never ends but when we stay positive on our hopes then God is also with us and good happens as we hope.

This story is from the time when the Covid-19 pandemic had just started. Many relationships started, two hearts connected, and two families met. But this pandemic played spoilsport—the enthusiasm and preparation of marriage in the family was greatly affected. Boy's name was Cheri and the girl's name was Angel and the date fixed by the elders in the family was 02/05/2021. Did everyone's hope shatter because of this pandemic? Yes, it did, except the boy's mother.

Cheri's mother Sadhana's hope was not broken, she was positive that this wedding will happen and started preparations for the long-awaited marriage ceremonies. Every day Covid-19 cases were increasing but Sadhana's hopes stayed afloat, because she had always dreamt of her son's marriage and wanted it to happen. The same dreams were also in the eyes of her daughter-in-law, Angel—who too wanted to see herself as a bride, and like any other bride wanted a big wedding with all her near and dear ones attending. She wanted gaiety, fun, dancing, and happiness all round. Angel was very worried about this pandemic. She constantly worried about her marriage—would it happen or not? And will her marriage be like others? Carefree from pandemic issues? Sadhana told Angel not to give up hope and pray for the situation to improve so that everyone could attend this wedding.

Everything was not going well, the government first gave permission for fifty people to attend the ceremonies, then seeing the worsening situation, reduced it to ten. Both the families were shattered. Ten guests only? They knew no other date was as auspicious as the one they had fixed on, and they so desperately wanted the wedding to happen.

Time passed.

28th April 2021

Pre-wedding rituals started, and the cases of Covid-19 also increased. The families dithered, as the government too. Both the families met but could not take any decision. As usual, Sadhana took charge and told everyone, that as there were hardly any cases in their village, they could and would go-ahead with the marriage. So, both the families decided that marriage will take place on May 2nd, 2021.

There were only family members in the wedding, no extra guests. Members of extended family felt left out and many complained. How can a marriage happen without guests, music, photographs, food a plenty? Where was the fun? How could Sadhana get her only son married like this?

Sadhana stood firm. She told everyone that this was the time to unite, and be with each other, maybe not physically, but definitely virtually. 'We will do every ritual with happiness, Cheri and Angel will get married, but we need everyone's blessings, so please bless them.' she urged.

After that, everything that happens in a marriage happened.

So, many people could not attend, so what? But they shared Sadhana's happiness in seeing her son getting married to the girl of his choice. Everyone was at peace, from that one hope of Sadhana and her determination for it to happen, came happiness in the life of all the members.

The time came for the procession, Cheri waved from their car, keeping safe distance. Everyone was happy. 'If we want something desperately enough, God makes it happen,' thought Sadhana. They reached Angel's house, under the police's watchful eyes. The whole wedding procession (ten people in all) was welcomed in the house with great respect. Rituals took place. A simple and heart-warming wedding happened.

Everyone had only one thing to say. It is not important to hold big weddings, and no point feeling bad that they could not invite everyone, but what is important is that the weddings should happen. The boy and the girl should unite. Rest everything else falls into place. If we do not give up hope, if we have a positive attitude, then no work is difficult for us, and we always keep ourselves calm and happy.

Life, Death, and Covid-19

@Prayash Gupta

Life, a lifetime opportunity to know life,
Sanctified creation of the Almighty.
But Humans, Drowned in deep abyss of the dodgy desire,
An immortal chase by the mortal being.
Anxiety, Addiction, Avaricious—utterly disregarding thyself,
In the crazy competition to establish thy identity
With the Herculean task of never-ending toil.
Consciously constructing happiness 'an occasional episode',
In the blissful life converting thyself to 'the drama of pain'.

Death, Life after life, a new dimension, a silent storm cellar,
Consciously enlightening Human, A tale of their mortality.
Otherwise ignored or baffled in their short but beautiful Life,
Scampering suppurating their super-phenomenon.
Snoozed in the labyrinth of apex avariciousness,
Deeming often the immortality of the mortal body.
Besieged by an inconceivable aspiration to conquer the planet,
Assassinating their peace, slaying their time in envy and giant
gluttony
Disregarding or ignoring their sole purpose of conquering thy
self.

Covid-19, An aide-memoire, A silent slaughterer,

Indiscriminately selecting lives to the expedition of life after life.

An invisible virus, Smaller than the smallest dot, travelling
throughout the globe,

Indiscriminately selecting lives to the expedition of life after life.

Not even giving an opportunity to know thyself,

An inconceivable arrest to the Human aspiration, Midas touch
and everything standstill.

Lockdown to the Human activities,

Doctors, Nurses, Cops, Scavengers, Front line workers

Staking their lives to save 'Humanity'.

An invisible virus, Smaller than the smallest dot, travelling
throughout the globe,

Indiscriminately selecting lives to the expedition of life after life.

The news coming in

A Rhino strolling on the empty streets, Dolphins returning in
canal water in Venice,

Elephants eating corn wine at Yunan province and sleeping in
the tea garden

And mountain range of Himachal visible from Jalandhar after
30 years,

Thousands and thousands of deaths, lakhs infected, while some
of them healed.

Quarantined, Majority locked up at their homes,
Some anxious, some frustrated, Some hopeless yet hopeful.
While Doctors, Nurses, Cops, Scavengers, Front line workers,
Staking their lives to save 'Humanity'.

The roads are abandoned, the chirping of the birds, the crowing
of the crow
Even the reverberation of the silent breeze is audible,
Otherwise, heard yet ignored in the busy mundane life.

Life, A lifetime opportunity to know life—Death, *Life after life*
Covid-19, An aide-memoire, people Quarantined
While their thoughts of Life, Death, and Covid-19
Ticking to and fro like pendulum of the old model watch.

This Tsunamis of Pandemic shall pass, Reminding Human of
life and death,
Millions of people stare outside their window, contemplating
their life outside
While the crows are outside staring at People, silent, shocked,
and serious.

'WE SHALL OVERCOME'
HARI OM TAT SAT

Meet the

Co-Authors

Nidhi H. Khasgiwale

Nidhi H. Khasgiwale, a fifteen-year-old student, is an art fanatic and a music buff by passion. She has been swimming competitively since she shifted to Mumbai. She practices yoga and lifts Kettlebells recreationally. She has swum with the gold squad at Thanyapura, climbed the Eiffel Tower, visited the Universal Studios, witnessed bullfights, and eaten egg tarts while travelling extensively with her family.

Nidhi was born in the Kingdom of Bahrain but presently lives in Mumbai with her parents and a younger sister.

Pooja Mandla

Pooja is an educator by profession but a word weaver by passion. She has a BSc in Medical, an M.Phil. in English literature, and a B.Ed. degree from Punjab (Chandigarh) University. She loves to read, write, draw, and travel. She finds inspiration from nature and the surrounding people. She is passionate about writing poems and is a regular contributor to several online platforms, where she has won many prizes.

Her poems have been published in 13 anthologies so far by various publishing houses, and a few are in process of making. Two of her poems have recently been selected for two different anthologies by an international press called Sweetycatpress. Her poems have also been published in international magazines like Literoma and Innsaei Journals. She has recently been awarded with the award of appreciation for the Annual Wordsmith Award 2021 by Asian Literary Society.

Donna Nongkhlaw

Donna Nongkhlaw is a wife and a mother of two shining souls. For her, writing is an escape from the hectic schedules of everyday life. It helps her search for her soul and look at the world with a different eye. Though she discovered the art of writing very late in life, she is ever grateful to have found it.

Ramya V.

Ramya V. is an IT professional who delves into the world of books, a voracious reader who believes the pen is mightier to bring about a change. She dedicates her time to writing stories and poems in English and Tamil. She picks her pen to write when she stumbles upon any

social incident, she feels needs attention. Writing fiction inspired by real-life incidents tops her list. In 2018, she also won the event 'Which quote of Mahatma Gandhi changed your heart' hosted by Gandhi World Foundation. She has contributed and won as a co-author to more than twenty-five anthologies in prose and poetry. Her works are regularly published on online sites such as Women's Web and Women's Web Tamil. She is also a recipient of the Literoma Author Achiever Award 2021. Her stories bagged a place in the top ten list of the 'Annual Micro Fiction 2021' contest hosted by Half Baked Beans under the categories 'Horror' and 'Erotica'. She received a certification of appreciation for her poem in the Annual Wordsmith Award 2021 hosted by the Asian Literary Society. She is also the editor of the poetry anthology "Anklets in my Hands". She also received the "Author of 2021" award from Author Pages for her debut book in 2021. She was shortlisted for the Orange Flower Awards 2022 hosted by Women's Web.

Kirti V.

An IT professional-turned-teacher, Ms Kirti is a busy mom of twins. The pandemic of 2020 brought out her writing skills. Apart from being a voracious reader across languages, she enjoys music, sports, quizzing, and drawing. She is a good orator and loves to recite poems. As an active participant in many online writing groups like Story Mirror, Artoonsinn, Asian Literary Society, Inkdew, Did You Write Today, Literoma, The Passion of Poetry, Penmancy, Poetry Planet, WriteFluence etc., she continues to learn the nuances of poetry, prose, and story writing. Her poems have been published in anthologies across languages. She has been nominated for the Orange Flower Awards for Poetry in 2021 and 2022. She is the recipient of the Literoma Author of the Year 2021 award. Her debut poetry book Tides of Life was published in January 2022. Her works can be read at www.kirtisignature.com

Col Gaurav Bhatia, PhD (Retd)

Col Gaurav Bhatia is a scholar warrior with an abiding interest in the field of Disaster Management and Disaster Risk Reduction. He has a doctorate, four post-graduate degrees in various subjects and has also attended the Executive Management Programme at the Indian Institute of Management (IIM), Lucknow.

Col Bhatia has published multiple papers in various National and International peer-reviewed journals, a technical book titled "Biological Disasters—The City Beautiful Un (Prepared)" and has also written for multiple anthologies. Post superannuation, he works in Public Health—operating out of Lucknow (Uttar Pradesh) as the State Lead (Immunisation) with Clinton Health Access Initiative (CHAI): William J Clinton Foundation.

Monika Patel

A firm believer in the idea that positive thoughts bring about positive changes, Monika practises the same thought and has experienced the same. An alumna of SNDT Women's University Mumbai, Monika has a bachelor's degree in Education with a specialisation in Learning

Disabilities. She is a learning specialist working with children facing learning concerns in areas of reading and writing. She has worked with reputed national and international schools in Mumbai. Monika discovered the joy of writing during the pandemic. Her stories, as well as poems, are drawn from her life experiences which have been varied and striking. Working on multiple anthologies currently, Monika also enjoys cooking, sketching and road travel.

You can reach Monika at monikapro21@gmail.com.

Hishita Lakhani

Hishita Lakhani is a young writer and blogger. She has always had a great passion for reading and writing. She is currently living in Dubai, and she recently started her own blog on Instagram and Facebook with the name 'Kgetskreative.' She writes quotes and poetry, and they are filled  with lots of positivity, inspiration, and creativity.

For her, writing is like her therapy, her go-to place, when she wants to be away from the chaos, in a totally different world; she takes her pen and paper and starts to pen down her feelings and her emotions. You can find it all beautifully written and presented on her page. She is forever grateful to God and everyone around her to encourage her to keep doing her best.

Apoorva Maheshwari

Apoorva is a software engineer by day and a writer by night. Though surrounded by computers for most of the day, she is an extrovert at heart. Her stories mainly stem from people and episodes around her. She enjoys exploring daily struggles and tough decisions through her stories. She also enjoys exploring nature trails and cooking.

Vivek Gulati

Vivek Gulati is a commerce postgraduate from Delhi University and holds a diploma and Marketing and Sales Management. He firmly believes in whatever is destined will happen to you. Being born to a Forest Officer meant living in tough conditions. Taught by his mother at home till class 1st as there were no schools nearby, he has seen how she supported his father in bringing up their children with the best possible education and values.

As an Advertising professional, he enjoyed writing ad headlines, ad copy etc. He started writing on topics close to his heart and the poems that came about have a fair share of his experiences. He has also written for two anthologies, 'Women Vs We Men' and 'Second Innings' for ILPH and 'The Marital Games' for Inkfeathers Publishing. The pandemic gave Vivek enough time to further develop his interest and he has off late contributed quite a bit on the online platform StoryMirror.com. His motto is to concentrate on quality and on topics close to his heart… *Dil se!*

Vasudha Kapoor Duggal

An alumnus of Loreto Convent Kolkata, Vasudha graduated in Political Science from Kolkata University and did her Management from IGNOU. She has a rich corporate experience of more than 25 years across 4 leading private companies and an MNC. She has worked in varied roles spanning different functions such as programming, EDP, Quality, Business Operations, and Marketing and she also spearheaded the SMB Direct Business and Contact Centre business of the MNC. She took early retirement from her corporate career to pursue other interests and also work in the social sector. She has three poetry anthologies to her credit and an e-zine where her poem was published. Vasudha now lives in Gurgaon with her family.

Manobhi Maltare

Manobhi is a pharmacist by profession and a writer by passion. In her free time, she likes to dance and read books and also devotes quality time to nature and pets. Her story Lockdown Wedding is her attempt to tell the readers that

the weddings as we see them in our culture have very less to do with those big invitations and lavish ceremonies. What matters is the peaceful and joyful completion of a marriage. If we don't give up hope and have a positive attitude, then nothing is difficult or unachievable for us.

Sandhita Agarwal

Sandhita is a software developer by profession but a hippie at heart. She likes to travel the world and meet different people. She completed her Masters in AI and ML from LJMU, UK. She is one of the authors showcased in the anthology Minds@Work2. When not writing or coding, she can be found listening to true crime documentaries and reading up on conspiracies. She lives with her spunky cocker spaniel in Bangalore and hopes to have a tête-à-tête with Salman Rushdie one day.

Arun 'Harry' Hariharan

Arun Hariharan a.k.a Harry, is an Indian Army veteran who switched over to corporate career post his military service. His over two-decade military career saw him foot slog in leech-infested tropical jungles of India's beautiful North-East, bash dunes in the scorching deserts of  Rajasthan, spot Red Pandas in the Himalayas and travel the world seeking adventure. An avid biker, compulsive traveller, photographer, and history buff, he's always loved exploring the unexplored. His collection of short stories titled "A Baker's Dozen: 13 Chilling Indian Tales of Macabre" which incorporated three of his passions—travel, history and exploring local legends—was published in October 2021 by Creative Crow Publishers, New Delhi. Besides, he has been a columnist with the Hindustan Times and the Hindu Businessline.

Arun is married to Kalpana, a passionate educator. They have two daughters and live in Gurgaon near Delhi.

Apurva Tandon

True to his life Mantra of *You Only Live Once*, Apurva Tandon lives each day to the fullest and describes his present days as his second life! In an earlier life in uniform, he served the nation for 24 years in the Indian Army before taking voluntary retirement in the summer of 2012 to explore a second life out of uniform and is now part of senior operational leadership in the corporate sector, leading global teams and dabbling in entrepreneurial ventures managed with the help of his wife.

Apurva is the bestselling author of "The 10 Meter Jump", an anecdotal account of his tumultuous transition out of uniform. He is also passionate about facilitating education for underprivileged children from the slum areas and actively works with an NGO on weekends for this.

A self-proclaimed lifelong student of the intricate human emotions, Apurva spends most of his spare time reading, listening to music and sometimes making music of his own.

Uma Bokil

A literate graduate who always wanted to work with books, Uma likes to read, write, and explore new genres of life. Her interests vary from food to nature to animals to what-not (The list keeps on growing). She currently serves as the Publishing Manager at Inkfeathers and thoroughly enjoys connecting with writers all around the world. You can find her enjoying the luxury of doing nothing on Sundays and getting cosy with a new book every now and then.

Vanshika Gupta

A postgraduate in Economics and a writer by feels, Vanshika hails from the UT of Jammu and Kashmir, India. In order to find the calm to her storm, she started writing her heart out and so writing about everything that she feels at her core became her meditation. She feels that words have a great power to inspire and to heal and if used in the right way, they can do wonders. She firmly believes in the idea of "hoping against hope".

Sanam Vaseem Shaikh

Dr Sanam Vaseem Shaikh is a lady with elegance, born and brought up in the small town of Bhiwandi. She completed her M. A. in English Literature from G.M. Momin Women's College, Bhiwandi, affiliated to the University of Mumbai and M. Phil from Allagapa University with an A grade in the year 2007. She presented a paper titled "Value Education" at a national conference held on 26th September 2015 in Shri Ram College of Commerce and Science, Bhandup. As of now, she is a teacher at Anjuman-I-Islam's Dr Mohammad Ishaq Jamkhanawala Girls' High School & Jr. College of Science and Commerce. She loves to adapt innovative methods to teach ALP (Accelerated Learning Programme) students. She spends most of her time writing and enjoying the little happiness life brings for herself. Her mantra is to live in simplicity and to ponder high.

Shirley Verghese

She retired as a banker seven years ago to a life of freedom from routines. Now was the time to explore and fulfil dreams and desires that were in the waiting. Rearranging her priorities, she now finds time for reading, travelling, and writing about her experiences.

She has spent the past few years of confinement during the pandemic by picking up online courses on a variety of subjects that interests her from Ancient History to Mythology, from English Literature to the study of Philosophy. She is a counsellor for those in need of support to rewire themselves and build their strengths.

Her journey with the Impish Lass in the past two years has moulded her writing skills to explore different genres. She has contributed to twenty of their anthologies so far, with articles, stories, and poems.

Uma Divgi

Based in Pune, Uma Divgi is an alumna of Lady Shri Ram College, New Delhi. She has a BA Hons Degree in Psychology. Enjoyed working in a travel agency post, graduation. She shifted base to Pune, Maharashtra after her marriage and spent 23 blissful years in a pre-primary  school. She takes keen interest in understanding people and the human aspects of life. She likes expressing her thoughts, though she has never written for anyone other than for herself. Inspired by a quote by Chuck Palahniuk, 'We all die. The goal isn't to live forever, the goal is to create something that will.' quarantine time actually gave her the opportunity to explore her writing skills.

Dr Anjali Dalal

Dr Anjali Dalal is a weaver of words and a teacher-trainer in her second innings. She holds a Ph.D. in English Literature. Anjali has spent a sizeable part of her earth life in the halls of academia. As a military spouse, she has styled her multiple homes and gardens. She is nearly an aficionado. @bungalowthirty9 is her recent passion project. Daydreaming, yoga, books, music, pets, and parenting fill her day. She is a tea snob.

Aditi Lahiry

Aditi is an English and French Language trainer. She is passionate about writing short stories, poems and articles mostly surrounding around Women and Children. She is passionate about storytelling too. Her articles and short stories have been published in Impish Lass Requiem and Women Vs We Men by Impish Lass Publishing House in 2021. She lives in Hyderabad with her family including her eight-year-old son, who, too, has a flair for writing short stories.

Pavan Revannavar

Pavan is twenty-two years old, born in Dharwad, Karnataka and brought up in Mumbai. Being in a normal conservative family, Pavan is with rich values and virtues. An honest and simple person, he believes in being kind and good to others. In a world where people run behind materialistic things, Pavan likes to live by intellectual and cultural values.

Pavan is an engineer by profession and a writer by passion yet very passionate about learning and has a keen interest in doing and exploring new things. A very joyful and easy-going person, Pavan enjoys being with family and friends.

Deepti Sharma

Dr Deepti L. Sharma holds a Ph.D. in Ecology and runs her environmental consultancy firm, but her heart lies firmly in writing. So, to summarise her in one sentence: She's married to science, romancing Literature!

Zeyd Ladha

Zeyd Ladha is an engineer, entrepreneur, and writer. Managing his factory by the day, he switches roles to become a writer by night. He is a keen observer and that is his major inspiration for writing. Writing articles, stories and poems with morals and teachings, he wishes to make a positive impact on the reader. His short stories and poems can be found on his blog and Facebook page, both by the name A Good Life.

Rudra Narayan Dash

If his life were a movie, it would not sell well. That's what being an engineering student is all about. Yet, Rudra Narayan Dash, student in the morning and writer at night, holds a special love for stories. For him, a story is not just a prose written to entertain or inform, but to spread a message in the most interesting way possible. Wanting to write since his childhood, he jumped at the first sight of opportunity when he was given his first laptop, and ever since that fateful day, he has written countless stories that are waiting to be uncovered from the depths of the endless tides of creativity. His unquenchable curiosity often puts him in a predicament about what genre to write about. But whatever he decides to write, he makes sure it is worth reading and sharing.

Prayash Gupta

Prayash Gupta is an Indian author, poet, and columnist. He was born and brought up in Pulbazar. His publications include "Ishwar Pick Up the Call", "Poetry Pilgrimage", and "The Gorkha's Story." At present, he is working as an Assistant Professor in Sikkim Manipal University. His biographical note has been included in "Asia Pacific Who's Who" (Vol. XV), "Famous India: Nation Who's Who", 2017 and "Learned India: Educationalists Who's Who", 2017, "Famous India: Nation Who's Who", 2018. He has been awarded "Best Indian Golden Personalities Award" 2017 by Friendship Forum, New Delhi, "Global Teacher Awards", 2018 by AKS Education Awards, New Delhi.

www.ingramcontent.com/pod-product-compliance
Lightning Source LLC
LaVergne TN
LVHW041140180726
843490LV00005B/1496